FLAMES IN THE WIND

The Undying Flames #1

LAUREN HANNEY

First published by Lauren Hanney 2021

Copyright © 2021 by Lauren Hanney

All rights reserved. No part of this publication may be reproduced, stored, or transmitted in any form or by any means, electronic, mechanical, photocopying, recording, scanning, or otherwise without written permission from the publisher. It is illegal to copy this book, post it to a website, or distribute it by any other means without permission.

This novel is entirely a work of fiction. The names, characters and incidents portrayed in it are the work of the author's imagination. Any resemblance to actual persons, living or dead, events or localities is entirely coincidental.

Lauren Hanney asserts the moral right to be identified as the author of this work.

Designations used by companies to distinguish their products are often claimed as trademarks. All brand names and product names used in this book and on its cover are trade names, service marks, trademarks, and registered trademarks of their respective owners. The publishers and the book are not associated with any product or vendor mentioned in this book. None of the companies referenced within the book have endorsed the book.

First edition

For Mam and Dad, who have always supported my love of books. Thank you for teaching me to follow my dreams.

I love you.

Contents

Acknowledgements

Chapter One — 1

Chapter Two — 8

Chapter Three — 26

Chapter Four — 47

Chapter Five — 62

Chapter Six — 76

Chapter Seven — 86

Chapter Eight — 95

Chapter Nine — 104

Chapter Ten — 115

Chapter Eleven — 127

Chapter Twelve — 141

Chapter Thirteen — 157

Chapter Fourteen — 172

Chapter Fifteen — 186

Chapter Sixteen	200
Chapter Seventeen	217
Chapter Eighteen	229
Chapter Nineteen	236
Chapter Twenty	243
Chapter Twenty-One	253
Chapter Twenty-Two	259
Chapter Twenty-Three	264
About the Author	

Acknowledgements

I never could have done this without all my friends and family, who supported me through the past few months and encouraged me to do what I do best: write. So, thank you to:

My mam, Sharon Hanney, for passing her love of books on to me, and providing honest feedback through the writing process. It's because of you that I wrote this book.

My dad, Mark Hanney, for supporting me and my dream to write a book, even if reading isn't your passion.

My siblings, Abbie and Jamie Hanney, because even though we sometimes don't get along or see eye to eye, you still showed your support and interest.

My friends, Chloe Mullen and Catalina Luca, for providing me with information to help ensure my book remained true to crime scene investigators everywhere and giving me honest feedback and opinions.

I really appreciate your help. I could never have done this without any of you.

CHAPTER ONE

His nostrils flared with anger. Everything was going wrong already. Though it was late at night, people stood watching the chaotic scene unfold before Him. Frustration boiled in His gut and pooled into His throat, a low growl gurgling to the surface. Nobody heard as they whispered in each other's ears, gossiping, questioning, wondering. He turned His back to the action and faded into the growing crowd on the street, disappearing before anybody had noticed He was ever there. He'd have to find another way to get what He wanted, and He'd stop at nothing to find it – even if it meant murder.

***

Catarina gazed at the cherry blossom tree dancing in the midnight air. It was a peaceful sight– one that brought a moment of joy to her night. A faint smile swept across her tear-stained cheeks. Blinding lights illuminated the crowded street as Catarina stood at the entrance to her house, watching, waiting. Years of pain, of sorrow, of fear. It was all over now. There was nothing left to be afraid of.

As the two officers of An Garda Síochána hauled her uncle into the backseat of their car, Catarina let loose a single breath, releasing all she'd suffered over the years, ready to live a life without constant fear of the man who had inflicted so much pain since she was five years old. As the car pulled out of the winding driveway, Catarina watched the flashing lights fade into the distance, until the only light that remained shone from the stars above. She stood there for several moments and listened to the silence that engulfed her home, people dissipating into the night, before she turned around in one swift motion, entered her house, and closed the door on her harrowing past.

Once the door was shut, Catarina leaned heavily against the doorframe, needing the support to keep her steady. She closed her eyes and took four deep hefty breaths.

One, two, three, four.

Alone.

She was finally alone. There was nothing to fear anymore. She opened her eyes just in time to see a big ball of black and white fluff jump up and wrap his front paws over her sleek shoulders.

Well, she was alone, with one exception.

Shep, a border collie just shy of two years old, stood gazing into Catarina's deep green eyes, a smile on his face and his tongue hanging from his mouth.

"Hey boy," Catarina whispered. She wasn't sure why she was whispering – it was probably out of habit from trying not to wake her uncle at night for fear he might be angry, or drunk, or both. Shep tilted his head in response, one ear sticking up, the other flopped at the side of his head. Catarina smiled for the second time that night. Shep smiled back as he leaned in closer and began licking the dried tears from her face. When no tears remained, he jumped down to the floor again and disappeared into the kitchen. As she wiped her face, Catarina followed suit, suddenly aware of her growling stomach.

She entered the kitchen to find Shep in his bed, curled up and already asleep. She envied his ability to fall asleep so quickly. Nightmares always followed when Catarina finally succumbed to the darkness of sleep.

There wasn't much food left in the kitchen. It had been over a week since she'd last gone shopping. Finally, after searching the near-empty freezer, she found a tub of ice cream with just enough left to satisfy her stomach until morning. She knew that she'd have to try and get some rest, but she also knew that it was highly unlikely to happen. It was true that her uncle was gone, and that he could never hurt her again, but that didn't erase all the painful memories etched into the back of her mind every time she closed her eyes.

***

Darkness embraced every shadow of the musty room. A heaving chest was the only audible sound, for silence clung to the stale air as if life depended on it. It smelled of rancid beer and spoiled food. Catarina's nose wrinkled at the foul smell as she eased the front door closed, flinching at the light creak it made as it shut. She glanced in the direction of the heaving chest that sat in a single leather armchair in front of the unlit fireplace.

He remained unmoving. Catarina released a single, trembling breath and tip-toed her way to the stairs five feet away, one uneasy step at a time. She tripped. Landing with a thump, Catarina held her breath and squeezed her eyes shut. She prayed that he was still asleep.

Please, please, please God, let him be asleep.

Silence fled as heavy footsteps thudded out from the room where he slept. Louder and louder, the floorboards groaned beneath his feet until silence emerged from its hiding place. Quaking, Catarina opened her eyes. Silence pleaded with her to run, but she remained frozen, lying on the bottom stair where she had fallen. A shadow stood tall above her, his angry blue eyes glaring down at her.

He was drunk.

"How dare you wake me up!" he shouted. Catarina felt herself shrinking, shielding her face with her delicate hands as he raised his own, preparing to deliver a painful blow.

She awoke with a start.

Beams of light shone through the curtains into Catarina's oversized bedroom. She groaned, turning to her side so that she could reach across and grab her phone from her bedside table.

7.30 a.m.

Sleep didn't come easy in the hours following her uncle's arrest. Her eyes watered at the thought of the nightmare – no, the memory – that haunted what little sleep she'd managed. She cupped her cheek in her hand, noting how it didn't burn hot from a delivered blow to her face, and gently pinched herself – a way to remind herself that she was awake.

Slowly, Catarina pulled the heavy duvet from her body and swung her legs over the edge of the king-sized bed. She rubbed her eyes, stood up, and headed straight for the shower. Ten minutes later, she returned to her bedroom. Her hair soaked and wrapped in a towel, she carefully decided what to wear – checked trousers and a jumper shirt, paired with low-cut black boots and – as always – her mother's locket. The round pendant felt cool in her hands, and she caressed the smooth lines of the engraved cherry blossom that covered the front.

Finally dressed and sitting at the vanity table, Catarina unwound the towel holding her dark curls in place and let them fall to her shoulders before applying oil to the tips.

"Now, where are my glasses?" she asked herself.

When Catarina entered the kitchen, Shep jumped from his bed and ran to her side.

"Good boy." Catarina smiled as she rubbed behind his ears, then padded over to the back door, unlocked it, and let Shep run free in the back garden. As Shep ran about, Catarina focused on pouring out his breakfast and finding something for herself to eat. With little else to choose from, she settled on leftover pizza from two nights ago.

Finally, at 8.20 a.m., there was a knock on her door.

"Come on, Shep," Catarina called out the back door, and Shep came running into the house, a trail of dirt at his heels. Another knock at the front door, louder than the last. Catarina froze, her eyes darting to the old oak door. Alannah wouldn't knock twice, let alone knock so hard you could hear the wood creaking from the force. Over the years, Catarina and her friend had decided that it'd be better to knock once, to ensure her uncle wouldn't be disturbed during his morning naps.

Catarina could feel her heartbeat quicken in her chest. She was acutely aware of a single drop of sweat slithering down her forehead.

It couldn't be. He was in jail.

The door handle squeaked, and Catarina gulped, struggling for air.

"Catarina Gallagher? Are you in there?" a voice called – distinctly male, and one Catarina did not recognise.

She crossed the kitchen quietly, beads of sweat now making their way down her whitened face. Silence had become her best friend over the years, when she had to be careful not to wake her uncle. Stealthily, she pulled a knife from the top drawer and clutched it to her chest. Her hands trembled in terror and her heart raced so fast she felt like she might puke. She made her way into the front hall, with Shep following closely behind.

A twist of the door handle paralysed Catarina where she stood, inches from the door. Shep let out a low growl, turning his body so that he stood between Catarina and the door. Her breathing quickened until her face was pink from panic, the palms of her hands so sweaty that she fumbled the knife and it fell to the floor.

Another knock followed by the *clicking* sound of an unlocked door. Catarina couldn't move. It was as if her feet were glued to the floor. The door swept open, and Catarina held her breath. She didn't know what to do.

Panic consumed her.

The man entered the house, and Shep jumped at him, teeth bared.

CHAPTER TWO

A garden of flowers lay on either side of a grand cherry blossom tree that complemented the garden adjacent to the momentous building. Noah gazed at it in awe. The building was vast and breath-taking – the stonework a work of art. As he climbed the steps to the front door of the grand house that stood before him, he cleared his throat, straightened his tie, and ran a hand through his hair. An old wooden door stood atop the steps. Once he reached the top, he knocked on the door.

As he waited for the door to open, Noah scanned the surrounding area, assessing each passer-by, noting the paths for escape should the need arise, and weighing the probability of an attack. Noah knew that this was not a requirement for the task at hand, but years of habit snuck up on him when he was least expecting it. So, satisfied with his assessment of no imposing threat at hand, Noah knocked on the door again – this time with more strength.

With no answer, Noah pulled the note with an

address scrawled on it from his jacket pocket. Margaret had given it to him before he left for Ireland. He compared it to the location portrayed on his phone, which confirmed that it was the right address. A quick glance at his watch told Noah that it was 8.25 a.m. The girl could be sleeping – it was still early in the morning, after all. Moments passed and still nobody answered, so Noah pushed on the door handle as he dug into his trouser pocket.

"Catarina Gallagher? Are you in there?" he called out. No answer, but he could have sworn he heard some shuffling from within the house.

Ah-ha!

Finally, Noah fished the single silver key from his pocket and fit it into the keyhole of the wooden front door. He turned the key until he heard the *click* of the lock and pushed it open. He'd only managed to take one step forward before a big ball of fluff jumped at him and knocked him to the ground. A blurred figure stood over him and... licked his face? Noah blinked several times and, when his vision focused, laughed, only to see a dog standing over him – chocolate-brown eyes glaring into his own.

"What the–"

"Wh-Who are you?" a voice asked. A small figure emerged from behind the door Noah had just swung open. His eyes widened, surprise evident on his face. Her skin was as pale as the corpses he had seen overseas, but she was beautiful – yet so quiet. Something fluttered in his stomach, but he couldn't identify it. He'd never had this feeling before. It confused him.

There was no denying who this attractive young woman was, with her dark curling locks and freckles that spotted her round face. Noah had seen images of Margaret O'Donnell as a child, and this girl was the image of her. It took him a moment to realise that she had spoken.

"Noah. Noah Thompson. I'm a friend of Margaret O'Donnell," he answered, still lying on the floor.

The girl's breath hitched, and her eyes widened; it was obvious she recognised the name. Noah reached his left arm around to the other side of his body, feeling for something in his jacket. The girl looked alarmed as he dug his hands into his pockets, backing away from him, further into the house. Noah pulled his passport from his jacket and held it up for her to see. She inched forward, stopping about two feet away. She had to strain her eyes to read the name on the laminated card.

Finally, with a look of approval and a glimmer in her eyes, she stepped back again and asked, "Why are you here?"

Noah's face scrunched up in confusion.

"Didn't you get the letter?"

Margaret had posted a letter to this address weeks ago, with an invitation to join her in America and enrol in the local university. He had thought that it was a very odd thing for Margaret to do. She hadn't seen her granddaughter since she was a child; they had only communicated through letters over the past several years.

Suddenly, she wanted Noah to cross the Atlantic to find this girl and bring her home to Athens, Ohio? But if Noah knew one thing, it was that Margaret O'Donnell was a truly unpredictable woman.

"I never got a letter," the girl said, snapping Noah's attention back to her once again. She stood for a moment; her eyebrows furrowed, and Noah noted how cute she looked when her little nose scrunched up in thought. "But maybe..."

She turned and took a single step back into the house, then stopped and smiled. Noah raised his head so that it was almost touching the dog's nose.

"That'll do, Shep," she said, and the dog standing over him was gone in seconds – back at the girl's side. Noah sighed in relief, now able to stand up and dust his clothes of dog hair. He grinned at the pair as he got up from the ground and followed them into the giant house, only going as far as the front hall, realising that he hadn't technically been invited in.

He watched as the girl shuffled through a pile in the cupboard under the stairs. Taking this opportunity to examine the house's floorplan, Noah shuffled towards the opening to what seemed to be the living room. After several minutes, the girl emerged from the cupboard, an envelope in hand.

"The seal is torn. My uncle must have opened it and hid it when he saw what my grandmother was offering me." With cautious hands, she pulled the letter from the envelope and began to read. A small smile escaped her pretty lips. She lifted her gaze from the paper gripped in her hands and met Noah's cool blue eyes, her smile matching his own crooked attempt.

"Noah Thompson; the man in uniform. Nanny did a good job at describing you, Mr. Thompson," she giggled, shifting her attention back to the letter in her hands.

"What did she say?" Noah took a few strides towards her, wondering what Margaret could have said about him to make this girl giggle so much, when suddenly she shrieked – though not loudly. It was more of a whisper than a squeal. She stretched out her hand and slowly backed away, her breaths rapid and her face flushing pink.

"Please don't," she gasped, her back pressed against the wall behind her. Noah stopped where he stood – mere inches from where the girl stood gasping for air, panic evident on her face. Her eyes were opened wide, her mouth agape and her chest heaving uncontrollably. Noah took three large steps back so that he stood closer to the door, allowing more air to fill the space between them. Flooded with concern, he wondered what he could have done wrong.

"Are you okay?"

She clutched something around her neck – a locket – and took four deep breaths in and out until her breathing was controlled and steady and nodded her head. She released the locket from her grip and let it rest on her chest. Noah raised his gaze to her eyes when she spoke.

"I just don't like people – particularly men – being near me. I guess you could call it a form of claustrophobia." It was obvious that she was hiding something, but Noah couldn't figure out what it was that remained hidden.

"Okay," he said. "Well, Margaret sent me here when she hadn't heard from you for a few weeks. She said it was unlike you to go without responding for so long. If you'd like to take her up on her offer to move to America, why don't you go pack and I'll wait down here?"

The girl nodded and asked, "How do you know my nanny?"

Noah's eyebrows arched at the term she used for grandmother but answered her anyway.

"She's old friends with my family. She always treated me as a son growing up. She was the only one who supported my decision to join the military."

His eyes shot to the ground for a second as he remembered how his family had disowned him for enlisting. His mother had always dreamed of him becoming a doctor and joining the family practice. He lifted his eyes to find the girl staring at him, but her eyes flicked away as soon as their eyes met. She nodded curtly at him and walked up the long staircase, the dog following at her heels. Noah couldn't help but chuckle as the pair disappeared around the corner at the top of the stairs, side by side.

Once he was alone, Noah began to explore the house, noting every exit, window and item of furniture placed around each room. As he entered the kitchen, hairs stood on the back of his neck – a prickling sensation crawled its way down his spine. Easier than he'd have liked to admit, Noah hovered his hand over the holster concealed under his jacket, his eyes sweeping across the room. A whirl of colour raced by the kitchen window. It was gone in less than a second, but Noah was already running for the back door.

***

Clothes of every shape and colour were scattered throughout Catarina's room – the bed, the floor, the desk chair. The sun still shone brightly through the window of her room, allowing light to pour into Catarina's idea of a new life across the ocean. Thoughts infiltrated her mind at a hundred miles a minute. Catarina's head throbbed in time with her pulse as she tried to think through the events of the past few hours.

In the space of nine hours, her whole life had changed before her eyes. She'd finally had her uncle arrested, meaning that years of pain could now finally rest in her past, and a stranger had shown up at her house, ready to bring her back to America with him. She sat on the edge of her bed, careful not to wrinkle her favourite cotton jumper as she sifted through her memories. Her newest wound was still fresh. She shook her head and unfolded the letter from her grandmother and began to read it again:

Dearest Catarina,

Your last letter was beautiful. You really inherited my talent for writing, and your description of your mother was adorning. Completely and utterly spectacular! It made me stop and think. How would you feel about joining me here in America and attending Ohio University? They have an excellent English program – you could minor in English and continue to complete the Master of Fine Arts Program in Creative Writing! It would be so wonderful to have you around in this big home of mine – it gets lonely at times.

Should you accept, I will arrange for a family friend to collect you immediately and bring you home to Athens, Ohio. His name is Noah Thompson (I like to call him the man in uniform) – quite a good-looking man if I say so myself. He can be a lot to handle so don't let those sparkling blue eyes and innocent smile fool you my dear, but he can be trusted. Noah is a loyal man, Catarina, and once he makes your acquaintance, he'll be sure to keep you safe. He's good at his job now, as most ex-military are, I suppose, so go with him and let him bring you to your new home. I look forward to seeing you soon, my dear.

All the best,
Nanny Margaret.

Catarina's eyes watered at the thought of a life in America with her grandmother. It had been so long since she had last seen her – at least fifteen years. Tears threatened to roll down her cheeks as Catarina realised one important piece of information: she'd never told her grandmother about her uncle – she'd never wanted to worry her. Catarina loosed a trembling sigh. She'd have to tell her now, since she'd have to return in a few months for the trial.

As she put the letter down on the bed, a picture sitting atop her bedside table caught her attention: a picture of her mother and father on their wedding day. Sparkling in the sunlight, her silk gown falling to the ground, hair tied back in a graceful display, her mother truly was magnificent. Catarina envied her beauty. Her eyes focused on the cherry blossom locket that sat firmly between her mother's collar bones, clutching it in her hand where it now hung gracefully around her neck. This locket was her prized possession – the only thing that remained of her mother after she and her father's plane had crashed somewhere over the Atlantic Ocean. A memory so vivid it could be real played before Catarina's eyes as she sat in her room.

A young girl – about five years old – jumped up and down on the giant bed. She looked so tiny in comparison to the mattress that she jumped on. A woman Catarina recognised as her mother walked into the room and laughed at the little child. The child jumped into her arms and they both collapsed on the bed, giggling up at the ceiling. The woman sat up and took something from around her neck. The little girl stared at it in awe, her mouth agape as she reached to grab it. The woman handed the engraved locket to her, leaned in closer, and settled it around the little girl's neck.

"This belongs to you now, Catarina."

That was the last time she ever saw her mother. Her parents had left that night for a business meeting in New York, and their plane had crashed into the ocean. There were no survivors.

Tears rolled down Catarina's cheeks as she held the locket tightly in her hand, not caring that the metal dug into her skin.

A thump from downstairs awoke her from her daydream. Shep leaped from where he'd been lying sprawled on the bed and out of the room. Catarina wiped her wet cheeks with the back of her hand and followed closely behind. She ran down the stairs into the hall and out through the kitchen to where the door stood ajar, Shep's shadow disappearing behind the wall. When she reached the door, there were two men wrestling on the ground and Shep was hopping around them, barking excitedly. One of the men – Noah – held the other to the ground, locking his hands behind his back as he pulled cuffs from his belt. Catarina's eyebrow shot up.

Cuffs? Maybe he's a detective or PI or something of the sort, she thought.

She stood anxiously by the back door, too afraid to go any closer to the men. Noah hauled the other man up to a standing position and pushed him against the wall with all the strength he could muster. He narrowed his eyes as he glared at the man.

"What were you doing in Miss Gallagher's backyard?" he asked, holding the man by the scruff of his jumper. He stood two inches taller, and Catarina couldn't help but notice how broad and muscular he was in comparison to the man in cuffs. He was an attractive man. Her face flushed a bright pink at the thought, but Noah was too occupied questioning the stranger to notice.

"I'm a journalist, okay!" the man finally admitted, turning his head away from Noah's piercing eyes. "I'm here to get her side of the story; Catarina Gallagher – the woman who put her own uncle in jail." His eyes darted between them frantically, hoping his answer would be enough for Noah to release him.

"I've answered your questions so please, can you uncuff me now? It hurts." He shoved his cuffed hands into Noah's chest and waited for him to unlock the cuffs that hung around his wrists. Noah looked to Catarina, a question on the tip of his tongue, but she was already rushing back into the house and had disappeared into the hall before he could say a word.

How could journalists know about the arrest already? It hadn't been a day since her uncle was hauled away in a police car. Catarina remembered the crowd gathered on the street – the whispers of her gossiping neighbours. She scolded her neighbours in her mind while she carefully folded and placed her clothes into the remaining two suitcases on her bed. In a small town like Dunlavin, gossip spread like wildfire.

When all her clothes were packed and ready to go, she decided that she'd send for the rest of her belongings as soon as she had settled into her new home, not wanting to have to pack everything right now. She was too eager to get on the road. Soon, she'd be with her last remaining family member. She'd be happy.

Just as she was about to leave the room, Catarina let out a short gasp and set down her suitcases. Turning back to her bed, she dropped to the floor and pulled a single drawer from under the bed. She couldn't leave without these.

The drawer was full of old mementoes from Catarina's childhood. A small photo album sat on the top of the pile, gleaming in the sunlight, a photo of a grinning child on the cover. Next to it lay a novel entitled "Flames in the Wind" by Margaret O'Donnell. Catarina scooped them up and held them close to her chest. These two little books were Catarina's version of her childhood in a bottle.

After a long moment, she unzipped one of the suitcases and gently folded the photo album within the clothes. She could never leave this – the memories of her family – behind. Once it was secure, Catarina put the suitcase on the floor and examined the novel. Her eyes scanned the cover; the silhouette of a girl surrounded by trees on a long road. It had been her favourite novel growing up and she'd hate to leave it behind. Deciding that it would create a satisfying distraction on the flight to America, she shoved the book into her handbag with a smile on her face. Finally, ready to leave, she looked over her childhood room for the final time.

How long would it be before she saw this place again?

She didn't know.

Memories flooded her mind – both good and bad: how her parents used to tuck her in at night when she was a little girl, and how they'd always read her bedtime stories; those nights after her parents had died and how alone she felt, with nobody left to read her stories. She was all alone.

With a final smile and a last goodbye, Catarina held her two suitcases firmly in her hands, exited the room, and closed the door behind her.

***

Noah uncuffed the reporter and led him through the house to the front door. He wondered what he had meant when he'd said, "the girl who put her own uncle in jail." When they reached the door, he pushed the man out of the house and watched as he made his way past the cherry blossom tree and down the driveway.

Good riddance.

He turned and saw the dog standing at the bottom of the stairs, looking up, waiting. He moved to pet the dog, but when his hand came close to his head, the dog growled and moved away. Pulling his hand back, Noah reminded himself that he was more of a cat person anyway.

"Sorry about that. He's very protective of me. Always has been. He doesn't like strangers very much," said a voice from the top of the stairs. With two suitcases in hand, the girl attempted to descend the wooden staircase; getting stuck halfway down, however, resulted in one suitcase slipping from her grip and falling to the floor. She chased down the stairs after it, examining the material to make sure it hadn't cracked. Her face glistened in the light shining through the open doorway. She had been crying.

The dog brushed against her legs, smiling up at her – a completely different dog to the one who had just growled at Noah. She ruffled the dog's ears and Noah noticed that she tried very hard to keep the dog between them. His eyebrows arched. What could have happened to her that she was this cautious of men?

"Is there something I should know, Miss Gallagher?" he asked, and before she could answer, added, "What's this story about your uncle the reporter was spouting off earlier?"

Catarina's breath hitched again; sadness coated her eyes. Nothing got by Noah. She focused her sad eyes on the dog as she clicked his lead onto his collar.

"I'd rather not talk about it right now, Mr. Thompson. And please, call me Cat." She spoke so quietly that Noah had to strain his ears to hear her.

"Okay," he said hesitantly, concern bubbling within, "but only if you call me Noah."

Cat looked up to meet his gaze, clearly

anxious though still very beautiful, and nodded. With Shep's lead in her hand and a suitcase in the other, she walked past Noah and out of the house, leaving her past behind her as she walked into the front garden. Taking the remaining suitcase in hand, Noah followed, closing the door to the old Gallagher home behind him.

Halfway across the garden, Cat stopped abruptly in front of the cherry blossom tree, staring at it in silence. Noah watched, glancing momentarily around him, observing their surroundings. Hairs prickled the back of his neck. Out on the street, a still shadow of a person caught his attention, but it was gone before he could examine it further.

"My grandfather planted this tree – the entire garden, actually. The cherry blossom is the emblem of our family crest." She looked to the locket resting on the palm of her hand. "I've always loved that tree…"

Noah noticed that Cat had stopped talking. Turning his attention back to her, he realised she was watching the wind blow through the rustling leaves of the tree.

"My parents and I used to have picnics under it every summer, if the weather was nice enough. I'll miss this tree."

The tree. She'll miss the tree, but not the house, Noah realised.

She looked at him and he noticed a single tear making its way down her cheek.

Without another word, she continued down the driveway to Noah's car.

"Can you open the boo-, er, the trunk please?" she asked.

Noah flashed a grin.

"It's okay, we call the trunk 'boot' back in Ohio, too. It's one of our many quirks." He winked.

A hint of a smile lingered on the corner of her lips as she watched Noah throw her possessions into the car.

Noah closed the boot, noticed Cat staring at him and flexed his muscles. Cat's rosy cheeks betrayed her, and she rushed to the car door. Noah laughed as he walked around to the driver's side.

She climbed into the passenger seat, Shep lying on the floor between her legs. She closed the door as Noah climbed into the driver's seat.

"You ready?"

Cat nodded her head, bidding her home of twenty-one years goodbye.

Noah started the car and she gazed out the window at the place she'd called home for so many years, remembering the picnics under the cherry blossom tree, until the car drove down the street and her house was out of sight.

***

He watched as the car drove down the street and out of sight. Both the man and the girl from last night – Catarina Gallagher – had gotten into it. Which meant nobody was home.

Though the street was empty, He kept to the

shadows of the overgrown hedges as He approached the vast building that was the Gallagher home. He went around the back, hopped over the stone wall and, just as He had hoped, the back door was unlocked. He must admit, the reporter had played his part. That so-called Detective Thompson had forgotten to lock the door after him when he was throwing the reporter out of the house.

Stealthily, He entered the house. He looked around at His surroundings. It must be here somewhere. If she were telling the truth, He'd find what He wanted in this house. As He rummaged the kitchen, He remembered the bittersweet sound of the pooling blood on the floor. Her final pleas as she begged Him not to kill her. A simple, deep cut across the throat – right where He knew He'd meet the jugular. She was dead in minutes. An eerie smile crossed His lips, and He moved on to the living room.

He searched every drawer, every cupboard, every shelf, and nothing.

He searched the dining room.

Nothing.

He searched the master bedroom. The wardrobes were empty, yet everything else remained. A single picture of a couple on their wedding day stood atop the bedside table and he grabbed it, but still, He could not find what He was looking for.

Anger bubbled deep in His throat, and He let out a low, terrifying growl.

Where was it? She said it'd be here.

Leaving the room, He slammed the door with such force the floorboards shook.

It wasn't here.

He left the house – now a mess – and clung to the shadows of the overgrown hedges once more. As He made His way to the end of the driveway, one thought invaded His mind: He'd have to pay a visit to Neil Gallagher.

CHAPTER THREE

The blurred shapes of buildings flew by the open window of Noah's SUV. Cat gazed out the window, admiration dawning on her face as each building zoomed by. Anticipation bubbled in her chest. Her heart warmed at the idea of a life here – in America. The wind blew through the open window, brushing against Cat's face in waves, sweeping her hair from her shoulders. Closing her eyes, she embraced the humid air on her freckled face. For the first time in a very long time, she was happy.

She could hear the constant humming of Noah's voice beside her as he drove through the streets of Athens, Ohio, but she was too busy closing her eyes against the gusts of wind, daydreaming about what opportunities her new life here would bring, to listen to him.

It was the American Dream.

When the wind suddenly stopped cascading across her face, she opened her eyes and turned to Noah, who smiled crookedly at her, his eyes gleaming.

"Welcome home."

An old-fashioned American-style house stood tall at the top of the driveway, a white picket fence outlining the property, which made Cat chuckle. It was so stereotypical. Leaning forward in her seat, she had to tilt her head up so that she could see the roof of the building.

Whoa.

Her heart leaped from her chest at the thought of calling this place home. What if she got lost? Sudden nerves raised the hairs on her arms. Though her heart had skipped a beat in joy, it now dropped to her stomach, causing her to grab her belly and wrap her arms around herself.

What if her grandmother didn't like her?

Sure, they'd written over the years, but she hadn't seen Cat in seventeen years – not since she was a little girl. She wasn't as pretty as the average American teenage girl was, and her grandmother was famous here. Surely, she'd prefer somebody who would look pretty in the magazine pictures.

Cat gulped.

Stuck in her seat, she didn't notice when Noah left the car, walked around to her side, and opened the door for her. Shep had already jumped out and was rolling in the grass, dirt sticking to his fur like pollen to a bumblebee.

"Aren't you coming?" Noah asked after a few moments, still holding the door open for her. She tore her gaze from the building that loomed over them and nodded her head once. Noah held out his hand, a gesture of goodwill to help her out of the car, but Cat hopped down on her own and walked over to where Shep lay in the grass, now a shade of brown from all the dirt that had accumulated on his coat. She didn't mean to be rude, but she just wasn't able to touch another man – at least not yet.

"Ready?" Noah had gathered the suitcases from the trunk of the car and was already halfway up the path when Cat took hold of Shep's lead and chased him up the driveway.

***

A cloud of frustration shadowed Him as He exited the police station, the man named Neil Gallagher following closely behind. He was confident that this man had the answers to the one question swirling around in His mind, but Neil's constant chattering ensured that He slowly lost the little patience He already had. The two men crossed the vacant street and approached the sole car that inhabited the car park. This man wouldn't shut up and it was driving Him mad. Anger rotted in the pit of His stomach. Slowly it climbed to His chest until He couldn't take it anymore.

"Get in the car," He ordered. The words came out in a low growl, but He didn't care. He wanted His answers and if this man didn't cooperate, He'd make him.

"What? No," Neil Gallagher replied, shrinking at the sound of the growl pulsing from the other man's throat.

He took one step closer to Neil and pulled back the right side of His jacket, revealing a holster at His hip, the grip of a gun sticking out from the top.

"Get. In. The. Car."

Neil shook where he stood and looked around him frantically, hoping somebody would turn the corner and walk into view. He could smell the fear sweating from his pores. It disgusted Him.

Men should not be fearful. They should be feared.

When it was clear that nobody was coming to the rescue, Neil climbed into the driver's seat, reluctantly shutting the door behind him. Thoughts buzzed in his mind. He could drive away before He got into the car, but by the time he'd come to the decision, He was in the car and pointing the gun at Neil's gut.

"Drive."

"Wh-where?" Neil asked, putting the car in drive, hands shaking as he gripped the steering wheel.

"Out of town. Follow the road until the houses become scarce and then pull into a big field on your right."

"O-okay."

Neil pulled out of the parking space and followed the road as he had been directed, glancing skittishly every so often at the gun aimed in his direction. He didn't say anything else until Neil pulled into the giant field in the middle of nowhere.

A single ruined building stood on the far end of the field, overshadowed by the overgrown trees falling over it.

"Pull in there," He pointed at the remains of

the old, abandoned shed. Neil drove over to the far side of the field and pulled into the remnants of the shed.

"Out," He ordered.

Despite the cool air trapped within the trees that covered the area, a nervous sweat collected at the nape of Neil's neck and slithered down his back, his shirt clinging to his skin. Before Neil could run, He pulled a zip-tie from His pocket and bound Neil's hands together then shoved him to the ground.

"Where are the bank account passwords?"

Shock crossed Neil's face for a moment before disappearing, fear taking over once more.

"What bank account p-passwords?" Neil stammered.

Anger cut through every word He said like a sharpened sword ready for the slaughter. "The passwords to the Gallagher family bank accounts. The ones with the inheritance money in them."

Neil's eyes flicked frantically around, avoiding eye contact with Him as much as possible.

"I don't know what–"

"Enough!" Anger erupted from His chest as He roared at Neil Gallagher. "I know that there are passwords somewhere and you know where to find them! Meredith Mills – or Johnson, as you'd have known her – told me before I took my scalpel to her skin and watched her bleed to death!" He had lost what little patience He had. He wanted those passwords and He wanted them now. No more messing around.

"Meredith? Why would you—"

Before Neil could finish his sentence, He'd pulled out His gun and held it inches from his face. Neil drew in a long, raspy breath, staring at the barrel mere inches from his forehead.

"Okay! Okay!" Neil squealed.

He huffed, shoving the barrel so close to Neil's head that an imprint was left on the skin when He eased it away.

"My good-for-nothing niece has them! Her name is Catarina Gallagher! I swear, she has the passwords!"

Neil released a quivering breath as the gun pulled away from his head, relief flooding his body. He turned His back to Neil. Finally, He'd gotten the answer he wanted, but He couldn't let Neil live. He had seen His face.

In the blink of an eye, He pulled a scalpel from His jacket pocket, swirled around and slashed Neil Gallagher's neck. Stunned, the man's eyes widened in horror as he fell back to the ground, red liquid seeping from the gash in his neck. His jugular had been cut.

He watched the life drain from Neil's body, a smile etching onto His thin lips. Pulling a crumpled tissue from His jeans, He took the necessary time to clean the blood-soaked scalpel. He'd be needing this again. A cool breeze shook the pool of blood on the ground, forming miniature waves. A sea of red.

Neil Gallagher was dead.

The car door shut behind Him, the only sound for miles. He drove along the field and back to the road, the smell of blood lingering in His nostrils. He inhaled, nostrils flaring, reminiscing in the metallic scent. It would take hours for somebody to find the body. As He pulled onto the road, a 'for sale' sign squeaked in what little breeze remained. He wished He could be there when the next group of buyers showed up for the auction.

The car sped down the road towards Dublin Airport. It was time He met this Catarina Gallagher.

***

An outstanding wooden staircase rested in the middle of the front hall of the house. Catarina guffawed at the spectacle. It was the exact staircase you would expect to see in the Titanic. Wood-panelled walls stretched down the hall, paintings hanging every few feet, from Giovanni Bellini to Leonardo da Vinci. Cat examined each one in detail, wondering if they were real.

"Incredible," she whispered, disbelief in her voice.

"Thank you," came a voice from behind her.

With a grin on her face and excitement coursing through her veins, Cat turned around to see her grandmother standing between a set of open double doors. Shelves of books lined the walls behind her. There must have been hundreds of books in that room alone.

"Nanny!" she squealed, running into the woman's open arms. Warmth flooded her. Being wrapped in her grandmother's arms reminded her of her brief time here as an infant. Her grandmother's arms wrapped tightly around her, and for the first time in a long time, Cat felt whole.

She was home.

Laughter rang through the room when Shep jumped on his hind legs, pushing against the two embracing women to keep upright. He looked from Catarina to her grandmother, tongue sticking out in joy.

"Well, who's this little bundle of joy?" Cat's grandmother exclaimed. Cat pulled away from her grandmother and watched with joy as Shep jumped up at her, licking her face as she rubbed behind his ears.

"That's not like him," Cat laughed. "He usually doesn't like other people."

"He doesn't like me anyway. That much was evident when he tackled me to the ground," Noah added, entering through the open doorway, beads of sweat glistening on his face – evidence of the humid afternoon heat and threatening a spike in temperature to come later in the day. He dropped Cat's suitcases where he stood and wiped his forehead, sighing heavily for dramatic effect. Cat stifled a small laugh, apologising once more for the misunderstanding.

Her grandmother smiled coyly. "Haven't you noticed dear, I'm a very likeable person." She looked down at Shep, who was sitting happily at her feet while she rubbed his head, not a care in the world.

"So I see," Cat said. She looked around the

front hall of the house once more, sneaking a peek behind her grandmother, attempting to see the room with the books. It appeared to be a library, or maybe a study. "This place is so beautiful."

Her grandmother appeared at her side and praised the painting that Cat had admired when she first arrived.

"It is." She looked to Cat. "Would you like a tour of your new home?"

Cat beamed. She hadn't been this happy in a very long time. Like a little girl, she jumped up and down where she stood, a large smile stretching across her face.

"Yes please!"

They hadn't even gotten four feet from the stairs when a thunderous buzzing sound echoed through the hall. Cat and her grandmother looked behind them, where Noah had been following silently, stifling their laughs as he rooted in his pocket for his phone.

"Shut up, shut up, shut up," he chanted as 'Dancing Queen' by ABBA rang in everyone's ears. Finally, he pulled the phone from his pocket and answered the call, his face pink from embarrassment.

"Sorry," he mouthed, then answered, "Detective Thompson," pointing to the front door and walking outside for privacy.

Once he was out the door, Cat and her grandmother couldn't hold back the laughter anymore.

"You are the Dancing Queen..."

The two women sang the chorus to the song

as they made their way to the first room of the O'Donnell house tour. Laughing so much they had to hold their stomachs and gasp for air, they entered the open kitchen area. It was absolutely beautiful.

Granite-topped counters lined the back walls; an island stood alone in the middle of the room, sparkling in the sunlight shining through the glass doors. Stools sat neatly under the counter of the island, the fridge a dark contrast to the white embracing the rest of the kitchen. The sink stood to the side, an open window atop it, facing towards a garden of sunflowers and daises.

"Whoa," Cat exhaled, finally catching her breath. She'd never seen anything like it before. It was otherworldly. The study was the same: beautiful, and something she never thought she'd have in her home. Sure, she had money herself, but she never thought of using it to build a house this big and this fancy. Her grandmother on the other hand, was known for this kind of thing. Her house had featured in several popular magazines over the years. If people didn't know her from her books, they knew her from this house.

At last, they reached the upstairs section of the tour. Standing at the top of the stairs, Cat wondered what her room would look like.

Would it be big?

What colours were the walls?

Would she be able to decorate it?

The rest of the house was so stunningly decorated. Would her room be the same? Anticipation built up inside of her. She hadn't been this excited for as long as she could remember. She felt the urge to run ahead of her grandmother and barge through her bedroom door, but she didn't know which door led to her room.

As if reading her thoughts, her grandmother asked her, "Are you ready to see your room now?" Cat just nodded her head, too excited to think of any words to say. "Follow me then."

Her grandmother led her down the long, brightly lit hallway. Two doors passed on the left, one on the right.

Which one was hers?

They stopped in front of an elegantly designed door. It was wooden, painted a dark brown – the type of brown you'd see on an old maple tree. Pink flowers spotted around the doorframe. Cherry blossoms. Cat reached out for the door and slowly twisted the handle, imagining what stood just behind it, then pushed the door open.

Her jaw fell open in disbelief.

Photos from her childhood decorated every inch of the walls – pictures of her parents, of her grandparents, of her. An antique desk stood by the window; a cushioned chair neatly pushed under it. The set was complete with a brand-new laptop and a vintage typewriter sitting on top. Cat's fingers itched to stroke the keys of the laptop and listen to the satisfying *ping* of the typewriter. She'd always wanted one, but the noise would irritate her uncle.

On her right, a set of cream double doors

stood askew, inviting her to see what lay beyond them. She entered the mysterious room to find a closet full of tops and shirts and jeans and skirts of all colours.

"I didn't know your exact size, so I got two of everything," her grandmother laughed.

Cat couldn't respond. Words caught in her throat, and she found herself unable to speak. This was the kindest thing anyone had ever done for her. She felt so lucky to be here – to have her grandmother by her side.

When she exited the closet, she noticed the bed sitting firmly in the middle of the room. It was by far the biggest bed Cat had ever seen. Even bigger than her own back in Ireland. Her eyes watered when she saw something familiar resting against the pillows.

"I can't believe you kept him," she sobbed. It was all so overwhelming: the photos, the gifts, and now this. She picked up the old, battered teddy bear from where he rested against her pillows and sat on the edge of the bed. Her grandmother sat down beside her, admiring the teddy bear clutched firmly in Cat's hands.

"I remember the last time I saw you; you insisted that I keep him here with me so that I would remember you forever. You were only three at the time."

"I can't believe you kept him all this time. I remember him. His name is Hendrick."

Cat pulled him closer to her and squeezed him against her chest. He had been her favourite teddy bear as a baby. He went everywhere with her.

Shep hopped up onto the bed and into Cat's lap, lying his head against the fur of the teddy. The two women laughed as they rubbed his head.

"I love it, thank you," Cat said happily. "And I love this place." She scanned the room again, taking in every detail.

"I should be thanking you for coming here to keep an old woman like me company. Books can only provide so much entertainment," her grandmother responded.

Full of joy and love and happiness, Cat and her grandmother headed back downstairs. When they reached the stairs, however, Noah came rushing back into the house, shoving his phone into his pocket as he approached the bottom of the stairs. He looked directly at Cat, who stood halfway up the steps. His face was a picture of concern.

"Catarina," he gasped for air, "it's your uncle. He was found dead eight hours ago outside of your hometown. I'm so sorry."

Cat's legs fell from under her. She reached for the banister beside her, her fingertips barely brushing the edge of the handrail as she began to fall. Quickly, she outstretched her arm again, this time gripping the wood of the staircase so tightly she could hear the wood groan under her grasp. As she held on, she clutched her locket in her free hand, counting to four, taking in deep, quivering breaths with each count. A comforting hand rested on her shoulder.

When she reached four, she looked back to

Noah, who had climbed the first few steps in an attempt to catch her.

"How?" she asked.

Noah's gaze shot to the floor. He was unable to maintain eye contact as he answered her question.

"It looks like he was murdered."

Her grandmother gasped beside her, startling her.

"Oh my!" her grandmother exclaimed.

The room darkened, clouds shading the world outside. Looming shadows descended over the house.

"What's going to happen now?" Cat said. "He doesn't have any relatives left in Ireland."

Noah's eyes shifted back up to meet Cat's, a coat of sympathy shining through the darkness.

"That's what I'd like to talk to you about. Would you mind coming back with me to the station so I can ask you a few questions? We can figure out the next step for your uncle's remains and everything you say to me will be sent back to the detectives in Ireland to help find out who did this."

Catarina choked back the urge to scream no. The thought of being in an unknown environment with dozens of men made her stomach clench, but she forced a single nod of her head.

"Yeah, sure, but can I bring Shep? I'd be more comfortable with him around." She looked to the dog, who sat happily at the bottom of the stairs, wagging his tail against the floor.

Noah hesitated, taking a moment to decide

whether the dog would be allowed into the station with her.

"Okay," he said finally, "but he has to stay on the leash at all times, and if he causes any sort of trouble – or even wags his tail the wrong way – he has to go outside."

"Okay," was all Cat could manage to say. Slowly, she descended the rest of the staircase and clipped Shep's lead onto his collar once more before turning back to her grandmother.

"We won't be long, Nanny."

She attempted a smile.

"I'm so sorry dear. I know Neil was the only family you had left in Ireland. He stood up to the responsibility for your care when my precious daughter and your father died. I will forever be grateful for that."

Cat flinched at her grandmother's final words, and though her grandmother didn't notice, Noah did. *He stood up to something alright, but it wasn't to care for me*, thought Cat.

"Thank you. I'll be home soon," she muttered, turning around and walking out the front door into the hot afternoon sun. Once she was outside, the darkness that had loomed over the house had disappeared.

Just as she secured her seatbelt in the car, Noah turned to face her, an interrogative look on his face.

"What happened with your uncle, Cat?"

Anxiously, Cat began to pick at her fingernails, avoiding eye contact.

Realisation hit Noah.

"You're okay now. You're safe."

Her lips began to quiver as she held back her tears, but as soon as Noah said those five words, she couldn't help but start sobbing.

***

Cat sat in the passenger seat of Noah's SUV, sobbing uncontrollably. Shep, sitting in between her legs, looked up at her with sad eyes.

"I'm s-s-sorry. I'm just s-so h-happy that he's g-gone."

Noah's eyebrows arched in surprise. He reached into the pocket of the car door, pulled out a packet of Kleenex and handed them to her with care.

"He hurt me. For years, he h-hurt me. I couldn't leave the h-house, or h-have anybody over or anything. For years I was isolated, b-beaten..."

Her voice trailed off then as she began to pull apart the tissue grasped in her hand. She glanced at Noah, then back at her hands. Gradually, she rolled up the sleeves of her shirt, revealing multiple burn marks spotted across her arms. They were circular in shape, small; the size that a cigarette would be. A look of horror covered Noah's face. The freshest burn only looked to be a few days old.

Another horrific thought crossed Noah's mind.

"Catarina, he wasn't... inappropriate with you... sexually, was he?" he whispered, hardly able to transform the thought into words.

For the second time in the space of ten minutes, Cat was holding her locket in the palm of her hand and counting her breaths. She looked up at him, horror evident in her eyes.

"No, he wasn't."

Noah slumped his shoulders in relief, releasing the tension in his body.

"Thank God. I guess that's why you have a fear of men coming near you?"

Cat just nodded silently, sniffed, and wiped her tear-stained face. Noah turned back in his seat and put the car in drive.

"And I assume you didn't tell Margaret either, given how she just praised him to high heaven."

A shake of her head was the only response she could give, bile churning in her stomach.

"Okay. Well, we're just going to go to the precinct that I work in, okay? I need to ask you a few questions about your uncle so that we can send the information back to the police in Ireland. I'll try my best to get you into a private room so you don't have to be around other officers. We have a few female cops in the precinct, so I'll ask one of them to keep you company. That sound okay?"

Cat released a wobbly breath and said, "Thank you, Noah. I really appreciate it." Noah flashed his crooked smile and Cat couldn't help but smile back at the handsome detective as he turned the corner and headed back towards the city.

FLAMES IN THE WIND

***

With the sun at its apex, the day was as bright as midsummer. He knew that He would not be able to successfully enter Margaret O'Donnell's house simply by walking through the front door. A small distraction would suffice, enabling Him to slip around to the open back window and climb through without anybody noticing.

Keeping His cap pulled low on His head and His hood pulled up, His face was completely masked as He handed some kid $30 to scream for help across the block. Successfully, the kid drew the attention of the passers-by and He managed to sneak over to the open window unnoticed.

As He climbed through the open window, however, a flowerpot dove to the floor. Anger boiled in His chest at the loud smashing noise it made as it shattered on the tiles, alerting the sole person in the house of His presence.

"Hello?" the woman called from the adjacent room. "Who's there?"

He approached the closed double doors that resided on the opposite side of the room.

"I'm warning you, I'm armed, and the police are on their way."

With a sudden sense of urgency, He rushed into the room to find the elderly woman by the table in the middle of the room, slamming a book closed and twisting to face Him in her chair.

"Where is Catarina Gallagher?" He demanded, frustrated at the fact that she was not there. He stormed over to where the woman sat and gripped her by the throat with His gloved hand.

"I'm not telling you anything," she choked, unable to breathe as He squeezed harder.

"Tell me where she is and where she hid the passwords!"

"Never."

She punched Him in the ribs with all her might, satisfied at the sound of His stifled groan.

He growled, pain searing across His abdomen.

"Then you're of no use to me."

He shoved the woman to the floor, still holding her by the throat as He pulled a scalpel from thin air and slashed at her throat.

Blood pooled from the gash in her neck. She choked on her own blood as she attempted to speak.

"You'll never get what you want."

With a bloody smile, she fell from the chair and landed on the carpeted floor, her eyes fluttering closed. She inhaled one final time, but the exhale never came.

Anger bursting from Him in short fumes, He screamed in frustration and kicked at the bookshelves beside Him until they collapsed to the floor. He turned for the door and fled the house.

Sirens echoed in the distance.

***

"Can't you drive any faster!" Cat shouted at Noah,

the blaring sirens drowning out her voice. Her heart was pumping in her chest to the rhythm of each siren.

Buh-boom.
Buh-boom.
Buh-boom.

The acid in her stomach swirled with each bump in the road the SUV met. Though she thought she might throw up, she urged Noah to drive faster.

A 911 call had come in ten minutes ago from her grandmother's address. Unable to comprehend the possible reasons for the call, Cat convinced herself that it must have been a mistake.

Her gut wrenched at the sight of numerous police cars pulled up outside the house.

Oh God no. Please. No, no, no.

Tears threatened to spill down her face, and she jumped from the SUV, Shep not far behind her. She ran up the driveway. People yelled at her to stop, to not enter the house, but she didn't listen. Her heart pumped so loudly; she could hear the *thump thump thump* of each beat in her ears. This couldn't be happening.

She ran into the front hall where she had stood only two hours ago, as happy as she'd ever been, eyes flicking around the room, searching for her grandmother. She'd only just got here. Her grandmother was the only family she had left. She had to be okay.

The whispers of voices sounded from the home library. She ran into the room, only to stop abruptly in her steps, a puddle of red liquid drawing her gaze.

The entire world slowed around her. Everything was at a standstill. Silence embraced her like a long-lost friend as her gaze slowly followed the trail of blood a few feet away, to where her grandmother lay on the floor – dead.

Catarina's stomach lurched, and she vomited all over the floor. She wiped the remnants of the vomit from around her mouth with the back of her hand and rushed to her grandmother's side, tears falling in waves like a waterfall on a rainy day.

CHAPTER FOUR

People swarmed around Cat as she sobbed at her grandmother's side. Blood pooled around her body; red liquid absorbed into the carpeted floor. Some of the people called out to her, shouting at her to get up, but Cat's cries drowned out their shrill voices. She'd lost her last remaining family member. She was truly all alone now.

Out of the corner of her eye, she noticed a shoe covered in blue film tapping against the floor. Her eyes blurry from the tears that blanketed her wet cheeks, she could just about make out the shape of a man towering over her. She shrunk back as the man lowered himself so that he was crouched down beside her, his gaze meeting hers.

Cat wiped her puffy reddened eyes with the backs of her hands, not realising she'd smeared blood across her face in the process. Her eyes trailed up and down his body again; he had blue film covering his shoes, gloves covering his hands, and he wore a jumpsuit of some sort. His face bore a mixture of sympathy and frustration.

"We need you to get up, Cat. You're

tampering with the crime scene," Noah said, trying to keep his voice calm. He glanced between where Cat sat on the ground and the puddle of vomit she'd left on the floor a few feet away.

As Cat slowly raised herself from the floor and her grandmother's lifeless body, she noticed a book lying on the floor. "Flames in the Wind" was scrawled across the cover. Cat picked it up and clutched it against her chest.

Voices shouted at one another from the opposite side of the room. People jumped back from where they stood, and one man lunged to the floor, reaching for something just out of his grasp. Shep dodged the man and ran straight for Cat, tongue hanging from his mouth.

"Somebody catch that dog!" the man shouted.

"Lie down, Shep," Catarina ordered, and he dropped to the floor. "Go back."

Shep got up, turned around and walked back out from where he had come running through the double doors.

"Good boy. Stay there," Cat praised him, and once again Shep plopped to the floor, wagging his tail, a giant smile on his face. He didn't move again, though his eyes remained glued to Cat.

The man who had lunged for Shep approached Cat and Noah determinedly, an angry frown on his face.

"Is that your dog?" He pointed a short stubby finger to where Shep now sat outside the doors.

"Yes," Cat answered, her gaze flickering to Noah.

"What's he doing here?" the man asked.

"He's my dog. He goes where I go," she muttered.

"Miss Gallagher, isn't it? I was informed by Detective Thompson here that you only arrived in America this morning. Why is your dog not under mandatory quarantine?"

The hairs on Cat's arms stood up, prickling her skin. She began to tremble, the heat of the man's breath sweeping against her face. It smelled of peppermint. Her gaze flickered to Noah once more, pleading for him to jump to her aid.

"I-I–"

Noah stepped between Cat and the man, acknowledging Cat's plea for help and forcing the man to take a step back, away from Cat's shivering body. She clutched her locket and counted to four, hiding behind Noah's broad stature.

"Sir, this dog is a support animal for the girl. I personally made sure that he went through all of the proper channels when we arrived, and we have proof of his vaccination within the last thirty days."

The man stared at Noah for a moment. It was as if his eyes were piercing into Noah's soul, Cat thought.

He grunted.

"All right, Detective, but if he even puts one paw out of line, I'm holding you responsible. Keep him away from the crime scene." With that said, he walked off.

Then it finally dawned on Cat what was

happening around her.

"Oh God, I'm so sorry Noah, I didn't think…"

Noah faced her with his big sympathetic eyes.

"Don't worry about it, but let's get you outside and let the experts do their job."

He led Cat out of the room, taking Shep along with them as they reached the double doors. They exited the house into the sunlit day. An ambulance waited outside, backed into the front driveway. Two paramedics hopped out of the front, and, at the sight of Cat's bloodied face and clothes, they hurried over.

"Are you okay, Miss?" the female paramedic asked.

"Is that your blood?" the male one questioned.

They bombarded her with questions, eyeing her clothes, her face and body. It took all her might to stop shaking as they led her to the ambulance, opened the back doors, and sat her on the edge of the platform, leaving the doors open for the fresh air. The female paramedic – she'd introduced herself as Maria – wrapped a tinfoil blanket around Cat's back while Noah spoke to the woman from the precinct a few feet away. She couldn't have been much older than Cat. Her deep green eyes revealed the horrors she'd seen in life, contrasting with her youthful complexion.

Cat's head was spinning – the world was spinning. What had happened? How did it happen? She had so many questions, but none of it felt real. She'd only seen her grandmother alive and well a few hours ago. She and Noah had only been gone for two hours.

When they'd arrived at the precinct, Noah had managed to find an empty interrogation room, away from the prying eyes of the other officers. He'd introduced her to his usual partner, Detective Evelyn Joy, who had sat with her while Noah talked to his Chief of Police. She was a very nice woman. She'd asked Cat about her locket, and she loved Shep. Then they'd asked her a few questions about her uncle – was he in any trouble? Did he have any enemies? The usual questions.

But now...

She was back at her grandmother's driveway and unfamiliar faces roamed the scene. People were gathering outside the yellow tape that had been put up, holding up their phones to record everything. Cat turned back to face the house and closed her eyes. Her stomach was uneasy. She felt like she might throw up again.

Somebody spoke up.

"Hi, I'm Jackson. I'm just going to take your pulse," the paramedic said.

He lowered his hand, reaching for Cat's, and she jumped back, pushing herself further into the back of the ambulance. Heart throbbing, she took heavy breaths as she screamed for Noah. The paramedic looked bewildered, not knowing what to do with himself. He tried to calm her down.

"It's okay," he assured her, "it's okay." He leaned forward, trying to reach her within the ambulance. She screamed, kicking her feet, trying to keep him away. Her breaths were coming quickly – too quickly – and she couldn't keep up. Beads of sweat rolled down her face.

A hand wrapped around the paramedic's arm and jerked him back, away from Cat and the ambulance.

"Can't you see that you're making her uneasy, panicked?" Noah yelled at the paramedic. "Take a walk."

The paramedic glared at Noah, anger in his almost-black eyes. His thin lips pressed in a tight line, he focused his glare on Cat.

"I was just trying to do my job!"

He threw his arms in the air and kicked the back wheel of the ambulance, muttering abuse to himself as he stormed down the driveway.

"Maria!" Noah waved over the female paramedic from where she stood talking to one of the forensics experts. She walked over, a pretty grin on her face. She glanced at Cat before focusing her gaze on Noah. She flicked her hair behind her shoulder.

"How can I help you, Detective?"

"Cat here isn't comfortable around Jackson. Would you please check on her? I'd really appreciate it." He flashed his crooked smile at the paramedic and Cat could have sworn she heard her giggle.

"Of course," she gleamed.

Noah turned to Cat.

"Maria will take care of you while I talk to Detective Joy. I'll be right back, okay?"

Cat nodded her head in response, silently wishing Noah would stay by her side. There were too many men around.

"I'm just going to take your pulse now sweetie, okay?" Maria asked.

Again, Cat nodded.

The paramedic rolled up Cat's sleeve until it reached her elbow, and let out a short gasp, covering her mouth with the palm of her hand. Cat knew what she saw: the cigarette burns. Neither of the women said anything as Maria counted quietly for thirty seconds, pressing two fingers against Cat's wrist. When she was finished, she rolled down Cat's sleeve and examined her clothes.

"Is this your blood?"

Cat shook her head.

"How about the blood smeared on your face?"

Cat's heart skipped a beat. Blood on her face? She shook her head again.

"Okay sweetie, I'm just going to wipe your face with a damp cloth, if that's alright with you?"

Cat nodded her head, eyes focused on the people in jumpsuits walking in and out of the house carrying boxes marked 'evidence', talking amongst themselves. Her vision blurred as her eyes watered. The warmth from the damp cloth brushed against her face, cleaning her of blood. Her grandmother's blood. She shivered, and the paramedic adjusted the blanket around her arms.

Noah returned from the house, clothes folded in his arms.

"Thank you, Maria," he said with a smile. The paramedic smiled back, nodded at Cat, and vanished into the house.

"I brought you these." Noah extended his arm, a pair of grey tracksuit bottoms and a hoodie resting over it. "I can't remove your suitcases from the house until the forensics team is finished with the crime scene," he explained further. Cat took the clothes from his arm, her fingers brushing against his as she did. She pulled her arms away and placed the clothes on her lap.

"Thank you," she whispered.

"You can change in the ambulance. I'll close the doors and make sure nobody comes near while you're changing," he stated.

Cat stood and backed into the ambulance, careful not to trip over the empty gurney. Noah closed the door behind her. Finally, the noise stopped.

The world was silent.

Cat's ears rang, a consequence of the buzzing noise of voices around her combined with the blaring sirens over the past hour. She tugged at her t-shirt, pulling it over her head and throwing it to the floor. She didn't want to see the blood stains. She'd cry again if she did.

Five minutes later, Cat hopped down from the ambulance, dressed in the tracksuit bottoms and hoodie. The hoodie was slightly baggy on her, but she didn't mind. She smiled at Noah. Detective Joy, Noah's partner, approached them. Though her face remained impassive, her eyes betrayed her emotion. She shot Cat a melancholic glance.

"Hey Cat, I'm so sorry about your grandmother. From what Noah's told me over the years, she was a brilliant woman."

"Thank you," Cat whispered, barely able to force the words from her throat.

"Do you mind if I ask you a few questions?" Detective Joy asked.

Noah stood next to Cat, trying to comfort her as much as possible without coming too close.

"It's okay if you're not up for it right now, but it may be better to get it over with," he assured her.

"I'll try my best," Cat said, her eyes focused on the gravel beneath her feet.

Detective Joy pulled a notepad and pen from her jacket and flipped it open.

"Did your grandmother have any enemies? Anyone who would want to hurt her?"

Cat shook her head.

"I don't know. We only wrote each other a few times a year. We'd just talk about whatever novel she was working on, I'd write short stories and send them to her, or we'd talk about the future – what my plans for life were. I've always wanted to be a writer. I wouldn't know if she had any enemies."

She looked to Noah, who spoke up.

"I knew Margaret O'Donnell all my life. As much of a cliché as it is to say, I never knew of anyone who'd want to hurt her. Her fans adored her."

Detective Joy scribbled in her notepad. Cat strained her neck, trying to see what she was writing. She looked up from the paper and met Cat's eyes. They were a deep blue. Her shiny brown hair made them glimmer.

"Nothing was stolen, as far as we can see. This is a nice neighbourhood, lots of wealth. Did either of you notice anything unusual – maybe someone who didn't look like they belonged – when you arrived this morning?"

Cat opened her mouth to respond, when Noah said, "No, I would have noticed if something were out of place." He stood tall with his hands behind his back. A leftover habit from his army days, Cat supposed. Detective Joy looked to her, waiting for a response. She shook her head for the umpteenth time.

"I hate to say it, but you only arrived today." Her gaze remained glued to Cat. Cat felt the urge to squirm, shiver, discomfort coursing through her veins, but she remained still, shoving the feeling deep down.

"Is it possible that somebody followed you here, entered the house under the impression you were inside, and found your grandmother instead?"

Cat's skin burned under the rays of sunshine. Was it possible?

"I-I don't know," she stammered.

Noah took a step forward, distancing Cat from the other detective.

"What are you implying exactly, Evelyn? That this is Cat's fault?"

Detective Joy took a step back, her brows furrowed, a scowl on her face. Her eyes flicked from Noah to Cat, then back to Noah. They stared at one another for several moments.

Finally, the detective's brows arched, her mouth ajar.

"Ohh, I see now." She smiled at Noah. "It's a plausible question, Noah. First, her uncle shows up dead after being released on bail, and now her grandmother is murdered?" Cat flinched at the word 'murdered'. "Death seems to follow Miss Gallagher wherever she goes."

Noah wrapped his fingers around the detective's arm and pulled her away from Cat. She watched the two, wondering what they were saying. They both wore scowls. Detective Joy talked with lots of gestures, pointing her fingers, waving her hands in the air. Noah ran his fingers through his hair. She couldn't hear over the noise of the crowd now gathered outside the front garden, a hum of whispers carrying with the wind.

Detective Joy pointed at Cat, her eyes remaining glued to Noah. Noah shook his head vigorously. Cat wrapped her arms around herself. She wasn't cold, yet her body still shivered. Detective Joy's shoulders slumped; her face resigned itself to a look of shock. She turned to look at Cat. The corners of her mouth twinged downward; her saddened eyes were directed at Cat's arms. Her eyes flicked up; meeting Cat's puffed teary ones.

"I'm sorry," she mouthed, and she walked into the house.

Once she had disappeared through the front door, Noah returned to Cat's side, his face a shade of red.

"I had to tell her about your uncle, I'm sorry," he said, his deep voice coated in pain.

"It's okay," Cat said, attempting a smile to ease his pain. Although he seemed to be a tough army man, he wore his emotions on his sleeve. "What happens now, though?"

The corners of Noah's soft lips lifted in response, the pain fading from his face.

"According to Evelyn – Detective Joy – a kid called for help around the time of Margaret's 911 call. He's being detained in a police cruiser down the street. I want to talk to him first, then talk to that crowd of people over there. There had to be people on the street around the same time as the call."

Noah and Cat walked down the driveway, Shep following silently behind them, and approached a police cruiser that sat on the curb on the opposite side of the street. Noah held up his badge for the police officer, who rested against the back of the car.

"Detective Thompson," Noah introduced himself, "I'd like to ask the kid a few questions."

The officer, who had straightened as soon as he had noticed the two walking towards him, nodded his head.

"Of course, detective."

He unlocked the car door and assisted the kid out of the vehicle. The kid's hands were cuffed behind his back.

Cat stifled a shocked gasp. The kid couldn't be more than sixteen years of age. Noah remained expressionless.

"I'm Detective Thompson and this is Catarina Gallagher," Noah said to the boy. "What's your name?" His notepad was open, his pen poised for action.

"Matthew," the kid responded, while his eyes scanned Cat's body – which was mostly hidden by the oversized hoodie – and he winked at her.

"Hey!" Noah barked, his voice husky. "Eyes on me, kid. How old are you?"

The kid jolted, fear seeming to radiate through his body at the sound of Noah's voice. Cat pitied him.

"Sixteen." He dropped his gaze to the ground and kicked the stones with the tip of his tattered shoe.

"And tell me Matthew, why were you calling for help earlier today?"

Matthew gulped, but remained silent. Noah looked to Cat, their eyes meeting for only a moment. Her eyes were still red from crying, so Noah flashed her his crooked smile. He looked back to the kid.

"Look Matthew, this is very serious. Something happened around the same time that you called for help. Someone was hurt. We need to know why you did it. Did you see something? Hear something?"

It was Cat who asked this, her voice soft. She crouched down, an attempt to attract the boy's gaze. His head tilted up just enough for her to see the tears threatening in his eyes.

Cat stood.

"Uncuff him."

She didn't direct the order at anyone in particular, but the police officer rustled the keys on his belt, looking to Noah, a quizzical expression on his face. He was asking for permission. Noah nodded his head once, eyes watching Cat.

"Thank you, Miss," the boy sobbed, rubbing his marked wrists. "Some guy paid me to do it – to scream for help. He gave me thirty bucks for it and, I-I needed the money. Mom isn't well. So, I did it and took the money. I mean, what harm is shouting for help for thirty bucks?"

"What did this guy look like?"

The kid shrugged. "I don't know, he was wearing a cap and had his hood pulled low. I couldn't see his face. He was taller than you, I guess, but not by much. I think his eyes were brown. The sunlight didn't reflect off them like they do Miss Gallagher's eyes." The kid smiled at Cat. A scowl darkened Noah's face.

"And when you called," he pressed on, ignoring the kid's obvious attempt at flirtation, "everyone on the street came running to see what was wrong?"

"Yeah, I guess so," the kid answered, not taking his eyes from Cat. Her skin prickled. His eyes reminded her of her uncle's.

Noah flicked his notepad closed with a swish of his wrist, satisfied, and tucked it into his waistband.

"Stay here. Detective Joy will be back to bring you to the station to answer more questions shortly. Do you have a phone? Can you call your parents to meet you there?"

The kid nodded, pulling a flip-phone from his pocket. Cat's brows arched. A kid without a smartphone was rare these days. Maybe he did need the money.

Noah ushered Cat away from the boy, back towards the house, and the crowd gathered outside the yellow tape perimeter.

"We need to question the neighbours," he said.

CHAPTER FIVE

Noah and Cat approached the group of onlookers and neighbours gathered outside the house. People stood crowded together, pushing to get a glimpse of a man pushing a gurney out the front door, a body bag on top. Noah positioned himself between Cat and the body bag, obstructing her view. This wasn't something she needed to see right now.

As they reached the crowd, Noah placed his two index fingers in his mouth, and whistled. Cat slapped her hands over her ringing ears, frowning.

"Sorry," he laughed.

The group adjusted their focus from their gossiping neighbours to Noah, holding phones and cameras in the air, recording the scene.

"Hello everybody. My name is Detective Noah Thompson." He held up his badge so that everybody could see. "Who here lives on this street and/or was present when the kid yelled for help earlier?"

A handful of people raised their hands, most of them in their early to mid-sixties, Noah thought. The same age as Margaret.

"What's going on?" one man asked. He was a short, rotund man with an angry face and no hair. "We heard there's been a murder."

Noah ignored the man's question.

"Can everyone who raised their hand please come with myself and Miss Gallagher here. Those who haven't raised their hands, this is a crime scene so please stay back or continue on with your day."

The few people who had raised their hands followed Noah and Cat over to the side of the street, whispering amongst themselves, away from the chaos of the crowd.

"What's going on?" the short man asked again.

"Please, quiet down," Noah ordered, as nicely as he could manage. He had to be careful not to anger any of these people if he wanted their full cooperation. "We just need to question each of you regarding the incident with the kid, the death of Margaret O'Donnell and the time the event took place," he said. "I'd like to question each of you one by one, if you don't mind."

Eight people surrounded Noah and Cat.

"I'll go first, I guess," the short man said, stepping forward.

"Okay then, Mr..."

"Harrison. Thomas Harrison."

"Okay then, Mr. Harrison. Please, step this way." Noah led Mr. Harrison under the shade of an oak tree and took out his notepad once again.

"So, Mr. Harrison, do you live in this

neighbourhood?" he asked.

"Yes. I've lived here for thirty-five years now with my wife and my two daughters. I knew Margaret O'Donnell. She and my wife were very close. We'd often have dinner in her yard during the summer months."

Noah scribbled in his notepad.

"And were you or your wife aware of anyone who might want to hurt Margaret?"

Mr. Harrison shook his head emphatically. "God no, she was the nicest woman I've ever met. Beautiful, too."

Lines creased Noah's forehead, a mark of surprise at the comment.

"I see."

"What were you doing at the time the kid shouted for help?" he asked, not lifting his eyes from the paper.

"I was washing my car," he said, his voice now shaky. Noah halted his scribbling and met the man's flickering eyes.

"Are you sure about that, Mr. Harrison? Remember before you answer, lying to a detective during a murder investigation would be impeding."

The man twiddled his thumbs and looked over his shoulder, making sure nobody could overhear him. Then he leaned in closer to Noah and whispered, "I was smoking, okay. Don't tell my wife, she thinks I quit years ago."

Noah rolled his eyes and stuck his hand into his jacket pocket. A laminated card rested between his fingers. He handed it to Mr.

Harrison.

"If you think of anything else, give me a call."

The man took the card and scuttled off down the street. Noah released an exasperated sigh and Cat stifled a laugh by pretending to be coughing.

Forty-five minutes had passed by the time they had finished questioning the final witness. Noah gave her his business card.

"I never thought that would end," Cat groaned. "That woman would not stop talking about her cats!"

Laughter boomed from Noah's chest, which attracted the attention of the woman who had just left their company. Cat turned her back to the woman so that she couldn't see the evident grin on her lips, which disappeared as soon as Cat remembered why they were talking to the woman in the first place. The pair walked back to the house. Most of the crowd had dispersed as the sun lowered in the sky, a cool breeze extinguishing the heat that had loomed in the air.

The people in jumpsuits exited the house, boxes of gear gripped in their hands.

"We're finished with the crime scene now. You can head inside. It's cleaned up for the most part," one of them called to Noah.

"Thanks," Noah called back, and they disappeared down the street in their vans.

Cat gawked at the mansion standing before her. A place that was full of happiness and joy just hours ago, was now coated in death and despair. Darkness loomed over the solid building, diminishing the light within. Noah remained silent for a few moments, allowing Cat the time to wallow; allowing himself the time to grieve too.

It was as if time had slowed down. A tear rolled down Noah's cheek, dripped off his chin and onto his shirt collar.

He sniffed, cleared his throat and said, "You shouldn't stay here tonight. It might not be safe, and the house is an active crime scene. I'll head in and grab your suitcases if you want to wait in the car. I understand if you don't want to go back in there right now."

"Thank you," Cat sniffed.

Noah advanced up the driveway. He heard the slam of the car door closing behind him and found that he was relieved that he could spare Cat any more unnecessary pain, even if it meant loading the pain onto himself.

The door clicked open, leading into the darkened hall. It appeared all light – all life for that matter – had been sucked from the house following the death of Margaret. The double doors stood ajar to his right. His stomach lurched. He felt as though he might be sick. Noah shut his eyes, entrapping the tears that threatened to fall, took a deep breath, and ventured up the stairs.

***

The door of the SUV closed with a bang, sending Catarina jumping in her seat.

"Sorry," Noah apologised as he secured his seatbelt.

"What's next for us?"

Cat focused her gaze on Shep as she massaged between his ears, avoiding eye contact with Noah and refusing to peer out the window at her grandmother's home.

"We'll need to check you into a hotel, for your own safety. I know of a dog-friendly hotel we can set you up in. Would you prefer to eat first or go straight to the hotel?"

Cat could feel Noah studying her, watching her every move. Though her stomach growled, as if on cue, the thought of food also made it churn. Bile slithered up her throat.

"Hotel first, food later," she muttered, swallowing the vile taste in her mouth.

"Fair enough." Noah turned on the ignition and pulled onto the street.

***

He tailed the car from afar, careful not to alert the detective and the girl to His presence. He kept himself at a distance, always maintaining two cars between the detective's car and His own. They drove back into the city. Evening traffic provided the perfect cover.

This time, He wasn't going to fail. He was going to make sure He got what He wanted. Catarina Gallagher was the last person who stood in His way, and she wouldn't for much longer, even if she had Detective Noah Thompson at her side.

The car turned onto East Park Drive and pulled into an empty car park. He read the brightly lit sign at the gate entrance: *Holiday Inn Express & Suites.*

A hotel? He watched from the side of the street as the detective, the girl, and a dog emptied the vehicle and walked into the hotel.

***

The doors swung open as Cat, Noah and Shep approached the hotel entrance. Tiled flooring stretched out as far as Cat could see, reflecting the luminescent lights on the ceiling. A comfortable little sitting area sprawled out on the right as they entered, pea green sofas separated by a wooden coffee table complementing the cream walls. An extended receptionist's desk sat firmly to their left, a beautiful young woman resting behind it.

Noah held up his badge for the woman.

"Detective Noah Thompson."

His husky voice was so attractive, Cat thought.

"Hello Detective, how may I help you?" The receptionist painted a pretty grin on her face, fluttering her eyes at Noah. Cat noticed how she glanced at her, casting her a disapproving look.

"I need one room, preferably on the ground floor, please."

Again, the woman's gaze shifted to Cat, and she could have sworn the receptionist scowled at her.

"Of course, Detective. A room for two, then?" She was fishing for information, trying to find out if Noah was available. Cat found herself amused, if only slightly, at how the woman's eyes scanned Noah's body, a tigress ready to pounce.

Noah, oblivious to the woman's flirtations, drew cash from a wallet Cat had not seen him take out.

"No, one adult and a dog."

The receptionist's grin grew wider – as if that were possible – her blue eyes sparkling.

"Sure thing."

Her fingers clacked away on the keyboard as she entered the information Noah offered into the system. When she was finished, she took out a key from the desk drawer and handed it to Cat.

"I'll be needing a key too, if you don't mind." Noah flashed his crooked grin.

This time, Cat was sure that the receptionist scowled at her as she handed a second key to Noah.

"You'll be in room two. Have a good evening." She said the last few words as she glared at Cat, before turning to Noah and putting her biggest attempt of a smile on her face.

"Thank you," Cat muttered, and they walked away from the desk in search of room two.

It didn't take long to find the room, but by the time they unlocked the door and got inside, Cat wasted no time in collapsing on the bed, her feet aching to be rubbed. Noah shuffled in behind her, suitcases in hand. She didn't hear him drop them when he said, "I'm sorry about Margaret."

Cat lifted her head from the soft pillow and met his gaze. She could just make out the tears that stroked his cheeks.

"I'm sorry too, Noah. You mentioned you were close. It's as much your loss as it is mine."

He sniffed, wiping his eyes with a tissue from the bedside table.

"Thank you."

Cat attempted a smile, but the muscles in her face struggled to comply.

"We will find out who did this."

Cat nodded, wondering if it was even possible.

Noah gathered himself, breathing deeply until he no longer shook.

"Okay. I'm going to talk to the receptionist, tell her that nobody is to enter this room except for me and you – not even the maids. We have to keep you safe in case the killer comes after you next."

"I'm going to shower and freshen up," Cat said. "Maybe after, we can get something to eat." Her stomach rumbled at that moment, and Noah stifled a laugh.

"I know the perfect place."

He walked out the door, leaving Cat alone for the first time in hours.

Everything hit her then. Waves of emotion rolled over her all at once, sadness, loneliness, grief, anger. She burst into tears. Shep padded over from where he'd been lying on his bed and cuddled into her, providing the only warmth in her heart.

"Thanks boy, I love you too."

Her grandmother's copy of her favourite book sat atop the pillow Cat had rested on mere moments ago. With delicate fingers, she picked it up and opened it to the first page.

My dearest Catarina,

I can bring tears to your eyes and a smile to your face. I form in an instant and last for a lifetime, but I can be forgotten. The answer is hidden on page six.

Love always,
Nanny Margaret

Cat released a breath, not realising she had been holding it in while reading her grandmother's final words to her. She covered her mouth with her hands, letting the book fall to the floor. She sat there, tears running down her soaked skin, wondering what it all meant.

***

The receptionist twirled her hair around her fingers as she batted her eyelashes at Noah. He tried not to notice, but she wouldn't stop. Sure, she was pretty, but Cat was much prettier. His cheeks flushed. He had just compared this woman to another person he barely knew, but he couldn't help it. Catarina Gallagher was a fine specimen in her own right. Though there was a slight age gap, he hoped that maybe, one day, when they had caught the killer and Cat had settled in America, he could ask her out on a date.

A sudden thought invaded his mind: would Cat return to Ireland now that her grandmother was no longer here? Surely, she'd stay, right?

The receptionist was blabbering on. About what, Noah didn't know. He hadn't been paying attention. He turned around, not caring that the receptionist was still talking to him, and headed back to the hotel room.

"Rude," was all he heard the woman say as he walked away.

Noah made sure to knock on the door before setting foot inside. He didn't want to walk in on a naked Catarina.

"Come in," Cat called from the other side of the closed door.

Noah opened the door slowly, peeking his head around it before opening it fully. Cat sat, fully dressed, on the large bed, her damp hair falling to her shoulders. He entered the room, paced over to the window, and pulled back the curtain enough for him to peer out, but not enough for other people to see inside the room. He scoured the car park. Besides the shadow of a car in the far end of the car park, there wasn't a person in sight.

"I've spoken to the receptionist; told her that nobody besides us are allowed to enter the room," he said, still looking out the window.

"She was flirting with you, you know. She kept scowling at me every time you looked away."

A smug smile crossed Noah's lips.

"Did she now."

It was a statement more than a question. Cat

focused her gaze on Shep, rubbing between his ears.

"Do you have a girlfriend?"

Noah's smile widened.

"I don't."

"Okay." She smiled.

***

Cat sat back in her chair and rested her hands on her stomach. She watched the cars drive by – people on their way home from work.

"That is the best dinner I've ever had," she breathed.

Noah winked.

"Good. Ciro is my favourite restaurant in the city."

Cat picked at her nails, not daring to look up as Noah called to the waitress for the bill.

"Noah, I need to show you something."

Noah's smile froze in place, slowly fading at the sight of Cat's expression. She hauled the book onto the table and pushed it across to him.

"Open to the first page."

Noah's smile disappeared as he read the message her grandmother had written in the last waking moments of her life.

"Cat…"

"I found it next to her body. I know I shouldn't have taken it, but she loved this book – she read it to me every night I visited her as a child, and I wanted something to hold onto that belonged to her."

"What does it mean?" Noah didn't look up from the page.

"I-I don't know, but it sounds familiar. She wrote it in her final moments, so it must mean something, right?"

Finally, he looked up. His eyes darted around him, and he slammed the book closed.

"She must have thought something was wrong. We should get you back to the hotel. We can talk about it there."

He left cash on the table and lifted himself up. "Let's go."

Alarmed, Cat stood and grabbed Shep's lead where she had tied it to her chair. They raced to the car and were on the road within minutes.

"What's going on, Noah?"

Fear coated her eyes as she strained to understand Noah's sudden rush to get back to the hotel. When Noah didn't answer, she twisted her entire body so that she could face him directly. Beaming lights blinded her through the side window, forcing her to shade her eyes with the back of her hand. The lights approached them at an irrefutable speed.

The force of the car slamming into them whipped Cat's head back against the window.

"Noah!"

The car skidded to the left, tyres screeching against the friction of the road, until it turned on its side. The *crash* sound echoed through Cat's ears as they smashed against the sidewalk, bumping against another car and setting off the alarm. Shep whimpered between her legs.

She reached out for him, her vision blurry. People closed in around the crash site, and Cat could barely make out the silhouette of the driver in the other car as it zoomed down the road and away from them.

Her eyes fluttered closed; her head throbbed. Something oozed from her hairline.

"Cat," a whisper came from beside her. "Cat, talk to me, are you hurt?"

Darkness consumed her.

CHAPTER SIX

A stampede of footsteps were the sole sound outside the room. Her nose crinkled, nostrils flaming from the smell of antiseptic invading her senses. A shuffling sound echoed from beside her, divulging the presence of someone else in the room with her.

"Cat?" Noah whispered.

Though her eyelids were heavy, they slowly opened. It took a few moments for her vision to adjust to the dull light. The hazy shadow of the man focused before her; concern etched his face. Noah leaned forward in his seat, cautious of his proximity to her body.

"Noah," Cat sighed, relief flooding her system, if only for a moment.

Between breaths, she found herself alert, searching the room frantically. She scanned every corner of the room until finally her focus shifted to Noah. He scooted closer, resting his hands on the side of the bed. Cat grabbed his hands, warmth shivering through her fingers, up her arms and into her heart. Noah's eyes widened, not knowing what to do with this newfound closeness, but he did not let go. Instead, he held her hands firmly in his own, providing comfort as best he could.

"Where's Shep?"

She was in a frenzied state. Panic strained her voice, her eyes darting around the room once more. She was never more than a few feet from her furry companion. He was her rock, her best friend.

Noah squeezed Cat's hands, drawing her attention back to him. She stared at the hands that covered her own, not realising that she had grabbed them in fear. Her head throbbed. It felt as though she were swaying from side to side. Noah stroked her skin with his thumb, a gentle reminder that she was safe.

"Shep is at the vet's. He's not seriously injured; his leg is sprained. The vet would like to keep him for a few nights to make sure it heals correctly, but he's going to need to rest for the next six weeks."

Cat blinked away the tears pooling in her eyes. She had cried enough over the past day and pain seared through her retinas. She loosed a shuddering breath.

"Thank you for making sure he was okay. I don't know what I'd ever do without him."

Noah offered a smile as she lifted her gaze from their intertwined fingers. Pain coursed through her temples. Black thread weaved its way through Noah's skin. She raised her fingers to trace the outline of the stitches at the edge of his hairline and stroked the wound.

"I'm okay," he assured her. "Do you remember anything from the accident?"

Cat dropped her hand back to the bed; she urged the memory of the accident to resurface.

"I remember a harsh light speeding towards us. Shep whimpered and I tried to reach him, but my head hurt, and I couldn't see him." Her eyes squeezed shut. She dove deeper into her mind, trying to remember what had happened.

"There was a man – I couldn't make out any distinguishable features, though. He drove away after crashing into us. Then everything went dark, and I woke up here..."

She opened her eyes and fell back against the plush pillows. Her temples pulsed at the side of her head, sending a shock of pain along her forehead.

"It's okay," Noah comforted her. "We'll figure out who this guy is and why he's coming after your family."

A polite knock on the door signalled a visitor, drawing their attention to a young man in a doctor's coat, a chart in his hand. Cat jerked her hand from Noah's calming grasp and heaved herself into a sitting position on the bed. As the doctor drew nearer, her breaths quickened, and her heart pounded in her chest. Finding it difficult to breathe through her nose, Cat sucked air into her open mouth, her head shaking rapidly, causing the pain to spiral out of control.

When he looked up from the chart, spouting off some medical terms Cat couldn't quite understand, the doctor noticed her hysterical state and ceased his advances at the foot of her bed.

"I'm sorry, Doc." Noah raised himself from the chair, keeping a tight grasp on its side to keep his balance. "Would it be possible to send in a female doctor? Cat here's just a little uncomfortable around men she doesn't know."

An understanding expression stretched across the doctor's face. He excused himself and assured Cat that a female doctor would be in shortly.

"I feel like I'm always thanking you."

Cat relaxed in her bed, allowing a minute smile to pass over her lips. Noah waved a hand aimlessly in the air.

"What are friends for."

Cat examined the man sitting at the side of her bed. She hadn't even known him three days and he was now the closest person to her in the world. She appreciated his dark tousled hair, ocean blue eyes and that crooked smile he was always flashing her way.

A short knock on the door followed by the growing sound of footsteps snapped Cat out of her thoughts, drawing her back to reality. She had been staring at her new, attractive friend, and he knew it. He flashed her that crooked smile and she almost felt her heart swoon.

Almost.

"Catarina Gallagher?" the new person in the room asked. She was an older lady with silver hair and a petite stature. She also wore a white doctor's coat and dark scrubs.

"That's me." Cat swivelled her head, lips still parted in a smile.

"Well, Miss Gallagher, you look quite happy for someone who was just in a car accident. Both you and the detective here." The doctor smiled at them both. Cat felt the warmth in her cheeks as they blushed a rosy pink.

"Nice to see you again, Doc." Noah waved, his chest rumbling from laughter.

"What're you in for now, Detective Thompson?" The doctor laughed, shaking her head in disbelief. She addressed Cat and said, "Noah here is always in here for one reason or another. The man finds trouble wherever he goes."

Cat whipped her head around, instantly regretting the action, to find Noah watching for her reaction.

"What can I say Doc, us military men are adrenaline junkies." His grin spread from ear to ear. He winked at Cat, happy as a pig in dirt.

When the laughing died down, the doctor flipped open her chart and read over Cat's file.

"Well, Miss Gallagher, you are one lucky lady. You managed to walk away from a car accident with a grade two concussion. Now, though the concussion is moderate, we still want to keep you overnight for observation." She closed the pages of the chart and met Cat's tired eyes.

"You may experience some possible confusion and/or drowsiness from the concussion. I'd advise that you try to stay awake for the next few hours. Our nurses will take great care of you and check on you throughout the night."

"Thank you, Doc." Noah stood and walked the doctor to the door, an evident limp in his step. They stopped outside the door, just out of Cat's earshot. Through the window, she could see the doctor nodding her head and then Noah shaking her hand. He popped his head back through the door.

"Coffee or tea?"

"Coffee please. Milk, no sugar." Cat yawned. "Stat."

***

Noah and Cat sat in the hospital room, stars from the inky night sky shining through the window, sipping their coffee.

"Just because I have to stay awake doesn't mean you do too, you know," Cat said between sips.

Noah sighed as the hot liquid seeped down his throat and into his stomach. Hospitals weren't known for their good coffee, but the caffeine still did the trick.

"Until we catch this guy, I won't be leaving your side. Whether you like it or not, you're stuck with me."

Noah winked. Cat focused her attention on her coffee, but Noah could make out her rosy cheeks in the dimly lit room. He smiled to himself, content with her reaction to his flirtations.

His smile faded and he spoke in a more serious tone, provoking Cat to meet his gaze.

"Look Cat, it's likely that somebody's after you. That car crash was no accident. The driver aimed straight for us. The fact that he knew exactly where we were is concerning. He was probably tailing us." Noah's gut clenched at the thought. He should have noticed somebody following them, but he'd let his feelings get the better of him and hadn't been focused enough.

"The chances of Margaret's death and the car accident occurring within hours of each other being a coincidence are slim to none. The driver, whoever he is, must have been following us for a while, which means the hotel isn't safe anymore." Noah drew in a deep breath. Because of him, Cat was hurt, and it could have been worse.

He closed his eyes, and an image flashed before him. A soldier – only nineteen years old – bleeding out in his arms. His eyes shot open. A look of worry on Cat's face reminded him of the boy. She reached for Noah's hands, but he pulled them away, tucking them beneath his legs, his breath heavy.

"Noah, what's wrong?"

Noah shook his head, taking deep breaths. It was just a memory. A dark cloud from his past.

"You're going to stay with me. I'll be able to protect you if someone comes after you." If he could put aside his feelings and focus on the job. Something he couldn't do in Afghanistan, and it had cost a man his life. "But, if at any time we need help, I have a few military buddies who could be here within the hour."

Cat's attention never faltered. She hung on to

every word Noah said.

"Okay. What do we have to do to catch this bastard?"

A smile stretched across Noah's lips. Catarina Gallagher was one tough cookie.

***

"Now remember, Miss Gallagher, if you feel even the slightest bit nauseous or dizzy, come straight back to the hospital."

Cat yawned as she scribbled her name on the forms the nurse had brought. She hadn't slept a wink during the night, and the copious amounts of coffee were finally wearing off.

"I'll make sure she's alright, if it's the last thing I do," Noah assured the nurse.

Bag in hand, Cat left the nurses' station and headed straight for the car park, stopping abruptly when she realised that they had no car. Noah's had been damaged in the accident and she hadn't had the time to go car shopping yet. Noah came out behind her.

"This way."

He turned to his right once outside the door and headed towards the closest vehicles to the front entrance.

"Evelyn dropped off my old SUV earlier this morning. It's not as nice as the other one, but it works just as well. It was actually a gift from Margaret when I first passed my driving test all those years ago." He chuckled, opening the door to the old Cadillac Escalade.

Cat's brow arched.

"How old are you, Noah?"

"I'm twenty-six. Young for an ex-Ranger, I know." Melancholy hung over him as he remembered his days in the military. "I injured my knee during my last op – needed surgery. I was medically discharged and came home on the next flight out of Afghanistan."

Cat inhaled.

"I'm so sorry, Noah."

Noah shook his head. "I lost a good man that day. It was my fault."

Before Cat could say another word, he closed her door and jogged around to the front of the SUV and climbed into the driver's seat.

"We'll head back to my house. I'll take the scenic route, make sure nobody is tailing us this time. You can get some rest and we'll visit the coroner tomorrow."

He cranked the ignition and drove out of the car park. Neither one of them said another word for the rest of the drive.

As daylight turned to dusk, Noah pulled into a small driveway.

"Stay here, I'm going to make sure the house is safe."

He hopped out of the SUV, eased his gun from its holster, and disappeared into the twilight. Cat observed her surroundings from the safety of the vehicle, though she couldn't see much, for a sole lamp lit the pavement outside of Noah's house.

Two minutes later, the passenger door swung

open, causing Cat to jolt in her seat.

"It's safe, let's go," Noah whispered.

Cat jumped down from the SUV and headed straight for the front door, Noah trailing closely behind. Once inside, Noah kicked the door closed behind him and jammed his weapon back into the holster at his hip and turned on a light.

Bookshelves lined the hall, packed with books from every genre. An opening to the living room on the left drew Cat further into the house. A dark leather sofa rested in the middle of the room, facing the unlit stone fireplace. A television hung above the mantle.

"You'll be in my room."

Noah led Cat up the stairs and into a snug room at the back of the house. A bed was positioned under the window, a dresser placed beside it. Some photos hung on the walls, but not many. The room lacked a personal touch.

Noah rested the suitcases against the wall.

"I'll be on the couch if you need anything. Get some rest, we have a long day ahead of us."

Without another word, he closed the door, leaving Cat standing in the middle of the room, alone. A door in the corner of the room guided Cat to a small bathroom. She unzipped her suitcase, removed a pair of pyjamas, and undressed. Using the small mirror in the bathroom, she tied her hair in a bun and brushed her teeth. Within minutes, with drowsiness weighting her body, she climbed under the comforter.

Her breathing eased into a rhythmic pattern, and sleep consumed her.

CHAPTER SEVEN

The wafting scent of food cooking on the pan flooded Cat's nostrils, forcing her eyelids to flutter open in hunger. Sunlight shone through the closed curtains of the bedroom window, brighter than she had ever seen before. She hauled herself from the soft sheets, fatigue hanging over her from a night of terrors.

Her feet trailed along the cold floor as she aimed for the bathroom. After a few moments, hot water soothed her aching limbs, washing away the dreadful memories that had resurfaced in her nightmares. Once she was sure she looked presentable enough for the public eye – and the eyes of the handsome man downstairs – she trudged down the stairs and into the small kitchen area where she found Noah hovering over the hob, in an apron, flipping pancakes.

"Good morning sunshine."

"Mmm," Cat groaned. "Too early. Need coffee."

Her zombie-like actions to the coffee pot resulted in a boom of Noah's laughter. Cat shot a glare in his direction, bringing the laughter to an abrupt end.

"Someone's not a morning person, I see." He plated a stack of pancakes, topped with bacon and eggs, and set them in front of where Cat sat at the counter, coffee mug glued to her lips. "Breakfast is served. I hope you like your eggs scrambled."

Cat arched her brow. Noah smirked, his cheeks burning red.

"It's the only way I can do them without burning them."

"How can you burn eggs?" Laughter entered Cat's voice as she tried to imagine blackened eggs. Noah shrugged, turned his back to Cat, and focused on cooking the remainder of his breakfast. Cat rested the empty mug on the counter and dug into her pancakes, one big forkful at a time. A moan slipped past her lips as the honey and nutmeg exploded on her tastebuds.

"Pancakes aren't as popular in Ireland. Our full Irish breakfast consists of eggs, beans, sausages, rashers – or bacon – with pudding, and toast." She stuffed more pancake than should have been possible into her small mouth. "But man, I love pancakes."

"You and me both." Noah grinned.

By the time Noah sat down to have his own breakfast, Cat was almost finished devouring hers.

"Wow, for a small woman, you sure know how to eat."

Cat scowled at Noah as she shoved the final bite into her mouth. She waited until she had finished chewing and had swallowed before she said, "Just because I'm petite doesn't mean I don't like to eat." Her attention returned to her now empty plate. "I didn't eat much growing up. My uncle always told me that if I got fat, no one would love me."

Though she wasn't watching for his reaction, she knew Noah wasn't pleased from the low growl sounding from his throat. Not wanting to talk about it further because of the painful memories, she changed the topic.

"What do you have planned for today? Visit the coroner, and then what?" Cat glanced at Noah. His facial features softened as he turned to meet her gaze.

"It's only been a day, but I want to check with the coroner and see if he has a preliminary report for us. Depending on what he tells us, I'll want to speak to some of Margaret's closer friends. I know she was part of a book club that met every Thursday at a coffee shop somewhere on West Washington Street. So we'll go there and see if they can answer some questions for us."

Cat finished her second cup of coffee and hopped down from the stool.

"Let me just grab my purse and brush my teeth and I'll be ready to go."

After brushing her teeth, she picked up Shep's lead and headed back downstairs. Noah was waiting by the door, ready to go. He flashed her a look of sympathy, nodding his head at the lead clenched in the palm of her hand. Realisation dawned over her. Shep wasn't here. She hung the lead over the banister, and they left, closing the door behind them.

***

The chilly air in the coroner's office washed over Noah's face, cooling him after the early morning heat. Though he embraced the cold air, he remembered the sombre reason for the use of the air conditioner in the vicinity: dead bodies.

The local pathologist emerged from his work area to greet Noah and Cat.

"Good morning, I'm Dr Andrews." He extended his arm and shook both Noah and Cat's hands firmly. "My condolences on your loss." He led them into a vast metal room. Noah's nostrils twitched at the smell of death and decay.

An outline of a body remained hidden under the fabric that coated it on the first of many autopsy tables in the room. The examiner rounded the table and faced Noah.

"I have completed my preliminary examination of Margaret O'Donnell. The official report will be handed over to the police department within the next few hours, though I can say with utmost certainty that my findings will remain the same." His empty gaze turned to Cat. "Do you know what Mrs. O'Donnell's funeral plans were, Miss Gallagher? She has you listed as next of kin."

Not knowing what to say, Cat shook her head and peered at the floor. The thought obviously hadn't crossed her mind.

"Margaret confided her funeral plans to me in case of her death over the years," Noah spoke up, catching the examiner's unexpected attention. "She wished to be buried alongside her late husband in Athens County Memory Gardens."

Dr Andrews nodded and assured Cat that her grandmother would soon be put to rest.

"Are you sure you want to see this, Miss Gallagher? It may be very emotional – she doesn't look how you remember her."

Cat nodded her head, tears already welling in her eyes.

He pulled back the fabric resting over the body, revealing Margaret's ghostly remains, a calm expression on her face. Noah's stomach lurched. He held his fist to his lips, willing the bile back down his throat. Though the bruises that smeared her skin were undeniably ugly, she looked at peace.

"What are your preliminary findings?" Noah choked out. He shifted his attention to Dr Andrews, though with every breath, he could smell death. Out of the corner of his eye, he saw Cat sniffling into her sleeve, wiping the tears streaming from her eyes. Noah stood next to her, as close as he could manage, and brushed his fingers over hers, a reminder that he was there for her. She took his hand in hers and squeezed gently.

She didn't let go.

"Well, it's obvious the attacker was wearing gloves. There's no alien DNA left on the body after the attack. There are signs of bruising between the C2 and C4 here on the neck, indicating she was strangled." He pointed a long-gloved finger at the bruised flesh, directing his comments at Noah.

"Now, it's a circular bruising pattern with a small diameter, signifying a hand grasped her around the neck and squeezed. Given that the bruising is light, he didn't have a grasp on her for long."

Cat sobbed, and Noah squeezed her hand, moving closer to her side.

"How do you know the attacker is male?" Noah took notice of the discolouration painted across his old friend's neck. It took all his effort not to gag.

"Good question, Detective. Given the size of the fingerprints, and the force and trajectory in which the neck was slit here" – he pointed to the stitched wound on Margaret's neck – "the attacker was taller and more powerful than the victim. This slashing wound on the neck is also the cause of death. The weapon sliced the jugular vein. She bled to death in minutes."

Noah knew he should be taking notes, but Cat gripped his hand so tightly, and he didn't want to hurt her any more by pulling away.

"I'd also like to point out the petechial haemorrhaging in the eyes." Dr Andrews placed a finger on either side of Margaret's eyes and forced them open. "The redness present here is indicative of a lack of oxygen – a result of the strangulation."

Cat pulled her hand from Noah's.

"I'm sorry, I can't hear anymore."

She hurried from the room, face in her hands.

Noah took a step away from the table, wanting nothing more than to follow Cat and soothe her in her time of need, but instead urged himself to listen to the rest of the information the doctor had to offer. The sooner they caught the killer, the better and safer Cat would be. He pulled his notepad from his pocket and began to scribble as the doctor continued.

"There's some slight bruising on the victim's thoracic and lumbar regions from where she fell." Noah flinched at the term 'victim'. "Finally, there is bruising and tearing on her right phalanges and the end of her metacarpals. She hit her attacker."

Noah paused in his writing and met Dr Andrews' gaze.

"Now, given the position she was in – from her angle and position on the floor with respect to rise of the chair she was in – we can estimate where on the attacker's body she struck, assuming he was standing over her."

"Where did she hit him?"

"My estimate: the ribs. It is very possible she bruised his ribs in the process."

A smile itched Noah's lip. Well done, Margaret. Noah thanked Dr Andrews for his help and left in search of Cat.

***

The girl came running from the building, hands cupping her cheeks, sobbing. She ran to a bench not too far away and dropped onto the wooden surface. She must have seen His handiwork. A contentious smirk twinged the corners of His mouth upward as He watched the detective rush out moments after her.

***

Cat sprinted from the building, eyes too blurry from sobbing to make out anything distinctly. She wiped her wet cheeks, spotted a bench a few feet away and fell onto it. When she could finally see again, she noticed two people approaching her at rapid speed. The paramedics from her grandmother's crime scene. A door opened beside her, and Noah ran over to her.

"Hey sweetie, you okay?" Maria asked, hunching down and placing a soothing hand on Cat's knee. Cat wiped more tears from her eyes and took four deep breaths.

She nodded her head.

"Yeah, sorry, we were just in with the coroner about my nanny," she said between struggling breaths. Noah sat beside her; worry smothered his eyes.

"Maria, Jackson." He nodded at the paramedics. "What are you guys doing here?" Though he listened for their answer, he focused his attention on Cat.

"Coroner's inquest. We're dropping off evidence for a case," Jackson answered, maintaining distance between himself and Cat.

"Oh sweetie, I'm truly sorry about your grandma," said Maria. "When I lost my grandma and grandpa, all I did was shop to keep myself busy." She jumped to her feet, giggling in excitement. "Tell you what! Here's my card, why don't you call me sometime and I can show you the best places to shop in the city!" She held out a personal card with her contact info printed on the white surface. Did everyone in America have these? Cat reached out and took it without saying a word and zipped it in her purse.

"We better get going now, Maria," said Jackson. "Dr Andrews will be waiting for us."

Maria hugged Cat, waved to Noah, and walked into the coroner's building.

"What now?" Cat asked, staring out into the car park.

"Well, the hotel is just down the street, so I say we grab your stuff before we head to the coffee shop so we don't have to come back later."

Noah stood and held his hand out for Cat, who took it with ease, and they headed for the hotel.

The reception was a pleasant relief from the heat of the day. Though no one sat behind the desk, Cat and Noah continued to room two. Noah pulled the key-card from his wallet and unlocked the door. Maybe Noah would let her rest for a few minutes, Cat thought. Sleep had not come easy last night. She pushed the door open, happy for the chance to rest her feet.

CHAPTER EIGHT

The once cream sheets were now a shade of dirty crimson, the result of the dried blood that had splattered from the remains sprawled across the bed. Her clouded red eyes peered into Noah's soul, sending a shiver down his spine. Once beautiful, the receptionist from the previous night, now covered in bruises, was almost unrecognisable, but for the name tag still pinned to her chest.

Noah remained frozen at the door of the hotel room, old memories resurfacing. Lost in his thoughts, it was only when he heard the startled cry that he awakened from his past. Cat stood at the bottom of the bed, hand clasped over her open mouth. Emotions flooding his system, the urge to pull Cat from the room and hide her from the danger of the world overpowered Noah, forcing him to take a step forward, into the revolting scene before him.

And another.

And another.

Until finally, he stood so close to Cat, he could hear her raspy, gasping breaths.

The air conditioner bustled loudly

somewhere in the background, banishing the heat that poured in through the smashed window. Cat pointed a shaking finger at the wall behind the bed.

She's dead because of you was smeared across the wall in large, messy letters. It was written in... blood.

A pang of guilt struck Noah's chest. Another person dead because of him. He scoured the room, seeking clues the killer might have left behind. He pushed the bathroom door open, checking behind the door and shower curtain – making sure the killer wasn't still here. His attention was drawn to the bathroom mirror, and fear expelled the guilt feeding on his conscience.

Catarina Gallagher, you're next.

He hurried from the bathroom, took Cat's hand in his, and dragged her from the room, back into the reception area.

"What's going on?" Cat demanded, pulling her arm from Noah's grasp and holding it close to her chest.

Noah's eyes locked onto her arm, suddenly realising what he had done.

"Sorry, we needed to leave. We couldn't contaminate the crime scene any more than we already had." His gaze fell to the floor. "Not if we want to catch this creep."

He took a moment, counted to ten, then pulled his phone from his jacket.

"Yes, this is Detective Noah Thompson. I have a 10-54d. I need officers and a forensics unit at Eleven East Park Drive stat." The call ended and he shoved his phone back into his jacket pocket. Cat sat in the lounge area, chin cupped in her hands, away from the prying eyes of the woman now sitting behind the receptionist's desk, clacking away at the keyboard of the computer.

"Excuse me, ma'am." Noah held up his badge for the new receptionist to see. "When did you arrive?"

The woman, much older than the previous receptionist, stopped typing and turned to face Noah, her glasses falling from the bridge of her nose.

"My shift started at midnight, why?"

"Where were you ten minutes ago? There was no one here when myself and my associate entered the premises." Noah clipped his badge onto his waistband.

"I was finishing my fifteen-minute coffee break. Can't a girl have some coffee when she's working the graveyard shift?" A defensive tone clung to the woman's aging voice as she answered each question.

"When you arrived for your shift, was the woman you were relieving still here?"

"What is this about, detective?" The woman peered at Noah; her cat-like eyes remained unblinking.

"Please answer the question, ma'am."

Sirens blared in the distance.

"No, she was not. I do not know where she was, to tell you the truth. Probably off with some guest somewhere. Now, if you will excuse me, I must get back to work. My shift finishes soon, and I'd like to have everything in order before I go." The woman reasserted her gaze back on the computer screen and continued battering her fingers against the keyboard.

Moments later, people in uniform filled the area, boxes of equipment in hand. As Noah led the experts to the crime scene down the hall, Detective Joy jogged up beside him.

"Tell me."

"It's the receptionist who greeted us last night. She's dead. Throat slit just like Margaret O'Donnell. Two messages left behind by the killer." He stopped by the door and turned to his partner. "He says he's coming after Cat next."

Detective Joy rested a soothing hand on his shoulder.

"You can protect her, Noah; I know you can. What happened in Afghanistan, what happened to Margaret, they weren't your fault. You're a great soldier. Cat's lucky to have you by her side." She smiled. "You obviously like her, so I know you'll never let anything happen to her."

Noah opened his mouth, ready to protest, but his partner cut him off before he got the chance.

"Go, protect her, find out who's doing this. But remember, report everything you learn back to me. This must be a professional investigation. Do everything by the book. I'll make sure everything here is searched thoroughly; no stone left unturned."

"Thank you, Evelyn. You're a good friend, and an even better detective."

He left his partner to do her part and joined Cat back in the reception area.

"Ready?" Noah cupped his hand in Cat's.

"Ready as I'll ever be."

The sun shined as they exited the building, climbed into the SUV, and drove in search of the coffee shop.

***

The aroma of fresh coffee swirled around the air. Cat relished the bitter scent that engulfed her nostrils as she took a deep breath in.

"Mmm, I love the smell of coffee." She grinned.

"Really? I couldn't tell." Noah laughed as he scanned the area. A group of women in their sixties sat at a bigger table in the corner of the room. "There they are." He pointed at the women. "Why don't you go introduce yourself and I'll order us some coffee."

When she arrived at the table, the four women lifted their focus from their books to her.

Cat's smile faded, nerves suddenly wracking her stomach.

"Hi, I'm Catarina Gallagher. I'm Margaret O'Donnell's granddaughter. I was wondering, are you the book club she was a member of?"

"Yes dear, we are. We were so sorry to hear about Margaret. Please, sit with us." One of the women gestured to the empty seat at the table. Cat slid into the chair and smiled at every member of the group.

"She was the glue of this group, always making sure we met up every Thursday, ready to begin a new chapter. We really loved her," another of the women spoke up.

"Especially when she gave us free advanced copies of her latest mystery."

The women chuckled.

Noah made his way over to Cat and the ladies. He handed Cat her coffee.

Laughter rounded the table as the women reminisced about some of the funnier moments in Margaret's life. Cat listened to each story intently, joining in the laughter when a story was told of how Margaret had once raced down the street after a motorcyclist who had called her an old woman.

When the laughter had died down, Noah asked his first question.

"Was there anyone who disliked Margaret? Maybe someone who was jealous?"

One of the older ladies shook her head.

"No, dear, we all loved her. I've never met anybody who had a bad word to say about Margaret O'Donnell."

The other women murmured in agreement.

"For weeks, she kept going on about how her granddaughter from Ireland might be coming to live with her. She was so excited." She smiled at Cat. "She really loved you."

Tears welled in Cat's eyes.

"Thank you."

The woman placed her hand over Cat's and smiled some more, fighting back the tears in her own eyes.

"She mentioned that she had something important to tell you – something about your parents."

Cat's eyes widened in shock; her mouth dropped open. Her parents? What could she possibly have had to say about her parents? They'd been dead for years. She turned to Noah, who nodded and thanked the ladies for their time.

"If you can think of anything else that might be of use, call me." He handed each of them his card.

Back in the SUV, Noah asked, "Do you have any idea what Margaret wanted to tell you?"

Cat shook her head. "No. My parents disappeared years ago somewhere over the Atlantic. I can't imagine anything she'd have to tell me now."

"We'll go back to the house after the funeral tomorrow. If she wanted to tell you something, maybe she wrote it down somewhere." Noah put the car in drive and headed towards the police station.

***

He watched as police cruisers and forensics vans drove out of the hotel car park. The girl had seen His piece of art, then. He'd get to her soon enough, and when He did, He'd get exactly what He wanted.

***

Cat greeted Noah as he climbed back into the SUV and slid files onto her lap.

"What are these?" she asked, counting each one.

"The files on the case so far; the coroner's report, crime scene reports, witness statements, evidence files." He buckled his seatbelt and pulled out from the front of the station and drove towards home.

"We can order some takeout and look over them tonight. The funeral is tomorrow. Margaret's body hasn't been released yet, but the service should be nice, and she insisted on only having family at the burial ceremony anyway. I think she was afraid of hundreds of fans showing up." Noah laughed quietly to himself at his late friend's worries and how extravagant they were.

Back at the house, Cat and Noah sat on the floor against the base of the sofa, eating Chinese and sorting through each file. For hours, nothing significant appeared, only information they already knew. Cat threw her chopsticks into the box as she flipped the page of the file on the 'unsub'. A comment at the bottom of the page caught her attention.

"From evidence shown at both crime scenes, the killer appears confident and controlled. Both victims display minimal defensive wounds. Each killing blow to the neck is concise. He's narcissistic. It is possible that the killer may return to the scene of the crime to witness the reaction of those who discover the bodies," she read aloud.

Noah took the file from her.

"Dr Lily Joy. That's Evelyn's sister. She's a shrink – sometimes she helps out on some of our harder cases and creates profiles for the perps," he explained.

"It says here that the receptionist led a man from the reception area further into the building." Cat leaned closer to Noah, indicating the paragraph she was reading from another file. "The man was wearing a baseball cap and a dark hoodie, just like the kid described when we asked him who paid him at my nanny's. Could it be the same man?"

She passed the file to Noah, who inspected the attached photo. After a few moments, he dropped the file on his lap, grabbed his phone from the nearby coffee table, and pressed number one on his speed dial.

"Evelyn, it's me. I have an idea."

CHAPTER NINE

Cat scanned the area surrounding the memorial service. People gathered from all over, an ocean of black spread far and wide across the park. There must have been over fifty people present. A sorrowful smile passed her lips at the thought of all those who loved her grandmother and had shown up to celebrate her life. It made her happy to know her grandmother was loved and surrounded by people from throughout her life. She turned her back to the growing crowd as the priest began his opening prayers.

Noah and Evelyn flanked her, keeping a watchful eye over the mass of people, looking for any signs of trouble, and Cat found herself thankful to have found people to share her grief with.

Everybody's attention shifted to the priest who now stood on the podium at the front of the crowd. Nobody noticed the plain-clothed and uniformed officers stationed throughout the park, sweeping the area for suspicious behaviour. A hand rested on her shoulder for only a second, a symbol of condolence. Cat smiled at her new friend and her partner and thanked the paramedics for coming.

When the prayers were finished, the priest began the service, his voice projecting over the crowd. People quietened their conversations, and soon the priest's voice was the only sound throughout the park.

"We are gathered here today to celebrate the life of Margaret O'Donnell. Mother, daughter, sister, wife, grandmother, and writer. She was loved by all, especially those closest to her. And she will be missed."

A gentle brush of skin against her fingers sent a jolt of warmth and comfort through Cat's veins. Relaxing her fist by her side, she intertwined her fingers in Noah's, thankful to have him in her life. His hand was much larger than her own. She felt safe. Tears flooded her eyes, flowing down her cheeks like a river flooding its banks.

After three-quarters of an hour had passed, the service was drawing to a close. Cat surveyed the area once more as the crowd dispersed across the field. People stopped by every once in a while to offer their condolences, but Cat wasn't paying much attention. The sun shone down from the clear blue sky. She squinted, wishing she had thought to bring sunglasses.

A tall tree shaded the green in the distance. A large man stood beneath it. He wore a dark hoodie and a baseball cap. Though glasses covered his eyes, Cat could feel his gaze focused on her.

Without thinking, she unclasped her hand from Noah's and took off sprinting across the park towards the man under the tree. A call behind her and a clatter of crunching leaves alerted her to Noah's pursuit. The man under the tree swivelled and sprinted deeper into the park. Not used to the strenuous exercise, Cat gasped for air and slowed, allowing Noah to pass by her and continue the chase. They disappeared into the trees.

Behind her, Evelyn, Maria and Jackson drew their chase to a close when they reached Cat, who was staring into the growth of trees beyond.

"Are you alright?" Evelyn asked, bending down to examine her. She placed a steadying hand on Cat's back, in case she were to fall over.

Cat nodded, gulping for air, her hands on her knees. She swayed, a sudden dizziness dawning over her. Maria held out a bottle of water for Cat to take.

"Here, drink this, it'll help."

Cat took the drink and downed half the bottle before attempting to straighten herself and nodded to her new friends. A few feet away, branches rustled, and Noah emerged from the trees, dragging the man by his arm, which was pulled behind his back, cuffs latched to his wrists.

"Let me go! I did nothing wrong; this is harassment!" the man spit out at Noah, dragging his feet along the grass.

When they got close enough, he handed the man to Evelyn.

"Take him back to the precinct. He knows something, I'm sure of it. We'll question him there."

Evelyn nodded her head.

"Come on, we have a cell with your name on it... whatever it is."

Cat watched intently as the police cruiser drove from the park and pulled onto the street.

"Is that him? Is that the man who killed my nanny?"

She refused to take her eyes from where the car had disappeared as she asked her question. A wave of emotions drowned out her senses.

"He claims to know nothing about it, but we'll get more information from him back at the precinct."

Cat pivoted, tears swelling in her eyes.

"He killed my family, Noah; we have to catch him."

"I know, sweetheart, and we will."

He wrapped his arm around her back, taking a chance, and pulled her against his chest. Cat wondered what it meant and, when she didn't pull away, Noah wrapped his other arm around her shoulder, lacing his fingers in her curly locks.

"I'll find him, if it's the last thing I do," he whispered in her ear.

They stood there a few minutes. Cat sniffed. Lavender and orange engulfed her senses and she pushed harder against Noah's chest, wishing she could stay there forever, where it was warm and safe. She surprised herself at the thought of feeling safe in a man's arms. His fingers nestled her hair in response, an attempt to soothe her.

It worked.

She released a shaking sigh and pulled away

from the warmth of his body. Her heart flamed at the thought of holding him again. She wished she could stay in his arms forever, free of the evil of the world.

A smile stretched across his cheeks, causing small wrinkles to form beneath his eyes. Cat wiped her own eyes with a Kleenex and attempted a smile.

"Let's get you home so you can change and eat before we head to the precinct."

The park had emptied in the time that Cat had been enveloped in Noah's arms. All that remained were a few dogwalkers and a family enjoying a picnic in the grass.

For the first time since she was a little girl, Cat realised that she felt safe in a man's arms. She had someone she could trust. From what she'd witnessed in the time she'd known Noah Thompson, he was an honourable man. Her grandmother was right, he was loyal, and once he got to know you, he'd do anything to protect you. She smiled as she remembered the comment her grandmother had made in that letter. She reminded herself that she must show it to Noah. He'd love to know what her grandmother had to say about him.

The pair walked side-by-side back to Noah's SUV and headed home to change before questioning the man at the police station. Hopefully, they'd get some information to go on.

***

A giant crowd gathered in the park for the funeral service, plenty of people to give Him the cover He needed to blend in. His decoy stood by a tree not too far in the distance, exactly where He'd instructed him to stand. It would be enough to separate the girl and Detective Thompson long enough for Him to get to her.

When the service ended, people began to disperse, allowing the girl the ability to see His decoy. Within no time, she was sprinting towards him, the detective at her heels. It didn't take long for her to tire, and soon she stopped, panting for air, while the detective continued the chase.

Now was His chance.

As He aimed for the girl, others stopped by her side, holding her, not moving away. He let out a low growl.

Moments later, the detective returned, His decoy cuffed at his side. He lowered His head and turned from the men. The female detective took the decoy from Detective Thompson and led him to a police cruiser. Having failed, He'd have to make a new plan – a plan where He could get the girl alone.

He left the park, annoyed, plotting ways to detach Detective Thompson from the girl's side.

***

"What were you doing in the park today, Mr. Brown?"

The man sat across the cold metal table. He

massaged his wrists where the cuffs once hung as he narrowed his gaze on Noah.

"I wasn't aware that it was a crime to go to the park nowadays."

Noah leaned forward in his seat and rested his hands on the table.

"Why did you run away from us when we approached you?"

The man threw his arms in the air, exasperated.

"You were chasing after me for no reason and you hadn't identified yourself as a cop. Wouldn't you run?"

Noah sighed, exhaustion from the day dousing his energy.

"You had the same descriptors as a man suspected of murder – dark hoodie, baseball cap. You're the right height."

The man leaned forward, his voice breaking mid-sentence.

"Murder? Look man, I just received an email from my online ad telling me what to wear and where to go. I didn't murder anybody. Oh man." He ran a hand through his hair, looking frantically around the small interrogation room. He shook his leg beneath the table.

Noah stifled a groan.

"An online ad. What do you do, Mr. Brown?" He arched his brow.

"I'm an actor. I post ads online and people hire me. You know, birthday parties, improv classes, those sorts of things."

"And when did you receive this email?" Noah

enquired, pen poised between his fingers.

"About two days ago. The guy didn't mention a name. I accepted the job and the next day there was an envelope of cash left on my doorstep." The fabric of his trousers shuffled as he shook his leg faster.

"Is this normal for you? People leaving cash on your doorstep after hiring your... services?" Noah shifted his gaze briefly to the paper as he jotted down the information.

"No, no it isn't, but I figured, there's no harm in standing next to a tree, so I took the money and did the job I was hired to do. I didn't know there was a funeral, or that I'd be chased by the cops. I wouldn't have done it otherwise," he babbled.

"We'll need your laptop, and the envelope of cash delivered to your doorstep."

"Of course, take them, anything I can do to help."

Noah stood from his chair and headed for the door.

"Look man," Mr. Brown said, scratching the back of his neck, "I'm really sorry about your, er... loss."

Noah ignored him and walked out the door, closing it behind him and entering the corner office. Cat sat at the desk chair, watching the city from the window. When she heard Noah enter, she swirled in her seat, eyes ablaze. Evelyn came in behind him.

"Well?" Cat asked. "Did he do it?"

Noah shook his head.

"No, but I believe the killer hired him to be

there, maybe as some sort of decoy.

"My sister is never wrong," Evelyn spoke up as she closed the door. "If she said that the killer would show up at the funeral, then he was definitely there."

Noah grunted in agreement. "The trouble is, we still have no idea who he is or why he's after Cat's family."

Evelyn turned to Cat. "Any progress on that message your grandmother left you?"

"No." Cat slumped in her chair. "But I plan on going through some old letters she sent over the years. Maybe there's something to find there."

Noah straightened, suddenly aware of his tiring posture, and yawned.

"We can look into it tomorrow. Let's get you home and into bed. It's been a long day; you need some rest."

***

Fatigue coursing through her body, Cat was relieved when she saw the porch light of Noah's house. She could practically hear the bed calling her name. Slowly, she hopped from the SUV and met Noah at the front steps to the house. She halted abruptly when she walked into Noah's outstretched arm.

"Stay here," he warned her, climbing the steps. Cat rubbed her eyes with the backs of her hands and watched Noah crouch down in front of the door. A small purple box sat neatly on the welcome mat, a white bow resting on top. With a gloved hand, Noah picked it up and examined it.

"It's addressed to you," he said. Cat followed Noah through the front door and into the kitchen. He set the box down on the kitchen counter and turned on the light, allowing for a better view of the gift.

"Stand back," he told Cat, who took a few steps away from the counter. Cautiously, he bent down and pressed his ear next to the ribbon. He eased the lid open and peered into the box. Releasing a slow breath, he called Cat back over to him.

"Have a look."

Cat peeked into the box, heart beating rapidly in her chest, curious as to what was hidden inside. She gasped at the familiar picture staring back at her – the one from her room at home in Ireland. The picture of her mother on her wedding day.

"There's a note." Noah pointed to the folded card.

"Can you read it to me?" she asked, searching for a stool to sit on. A static sound rung in her ears and her head felt light. Her empty stomach churned. The room began to sway. He had been in her house – her room.

Noah picked up the note from the box and began to read: *"You have something I want, Catarina – something that belongs to me. Give me the passwords, or next time, I'll kill that Detective Thompson you seem to love so much. You have seventy-two hours. Time's ticking."*

"Passwords? What passwords? I have no clue what he's on about, Noah," Cat panted.

Noah rushed to her side just in time as she swayed, almost falling from the stool she sat on.

"Okay, it's okay. Breathe, sweetheart, breathe. That's it."

After a few moments, when Cat had calmed down, he took a seat next to her and held her hand.

"We'll figure this out. I promise."

"But he said–"

"It doesn't matter what he said, we'll unravel the mystery and catch this guy. Hey." He lifted her chin up and met her disheartened eyes. "Don't worry about me. I can protect myself. I can protect the both of us."

He hoped. If he couldn't, he'd have no choice but to call in reinforcements.

They moved to the sofa, where Noah held Cat in his arms until she fell asleep. Her even breaths soothed his own. He held her all night, until dusk turned to dawn, watching over her. He'd never let anything happen to her. He couldn't live with himself if he lost another person he'd come to love.

CHAPTER TEN

Cat sipped the hot, bitter liquid from a mug, watching the small forensics team dust the box from the comfort of the plush sofa, her eyes following each stroke of the brush against the powder now coating the decorated cardboard. Still half asleep, her back ached from her night spent on the sofa. Though she had to admit, Noah made for a very comfortable pillow. For the first time in a long time, she hadn't had any nightmares.

Noah stood with the forensics team, directing them where to go and what to look for around the porch. One of the men offered a spiteful glare in Noah's direction, irritated by the constant orders. He turned his glare to Cat, who pretended not to notice as she continued to sip from her mug. One thing she had noticed more and more each day, though, was the detective's rugged handsomeness.

Time went by, and Cat watched the experts work, until eventually, the house was empty once again. Silence danced in the air while Noah poured coffee into his own mug, topped up Cat's, and fell back into the sofa, relieved to take the weight off his injured knee. He dragged a hand over his face.

Cat spoke first: "We have no evidence – no way – to figure out who this guy is. Where do we go from here?" she asked.

"We try and figure out why he's killing people and, hopefully, that will lead us to who he is. Do you still have the book with the message in it?"

Cat nodded and began to pull the book from the bag resting on the floor beside her.

"I haven't had the time to examine it properly yet though."

"Bring it with you, along with the letters Margaret sent you over the years, if you have them." He stood up and stretched out his arms. The bottom of his shirt lifted from the waistband of his trousers, revealing his well-toned abdomen. Cat risked a prolonged stare at the detective's olive skin and reddened when he noticed her eyes transfixed on his body.

"I'll go shower and grab the letters. Give me fifteen minutes." She rushed for the stairs, desperate to escape the embarrassment sprouting within her.

Cat's muscles relaxed as the hot water massaged her shoulders. Within minutes, she was showered, dressed and ready to go. Not caring about her wet hair dripping on her shoulders, she tied it in a bun and left it to dry.

"Where are we going, by the way?" she asked Noah when she reached the bottom of the stairs.

"Out for breakfast. My treat. We don't have any leads yet and it'll be good to get out of the house." He opened the door of the SUV and helped Cat climb into her seat.

The drive to the diner wasn't long, even with the thunderous rain forcing people to their cars. Cat had to admit, it was a nice change to always eating at home. She had rarely – if ever – got to eat out when she lived with her uncle. She slid into the booth, across from Noah, and picked up the menu that was set out on the table by the waitress.

"Can I get you anything to drink, honey?" the waitress asked.

"Coffee please," Cat chirped, even though she'd already had two cups that morning. When the waitress left to greet her other customers, Cat turned back to face a smiling Noah.

"Remind me to always keep a stash of coffee in my kitchen."

Cat nodded as she focused on the menu. So, the detective thought she'd be spending enough time in his kitchen to keep a stash of coffee in his house. Interesting.

Her stomach roared, begging for food, and soon. When the waitress returned with their coffees, they were ready to order.

"I'll have the biggest stack of pancakes you can manage." Cat said.

"Okay then." She scribbled in her small notebook, shifted to Noah, and before she could ask the question again, he grinned.

"I'll have the same."

"Two large stacks of pancakes coming up."

Cat watched the waitress disappear behind

the counter.

"People are always surprised by how much I eat. Just because I'm small doesn't mean I don't like my food," she said, propping her elbows on the table and sitting her head on the palm of her hand. She sighed and stared out the window.

"It's so different here to Ireland. The food, the people, the city. Ireland used to be my home, even if I didn't have a loving family for the better half of my life. Coming here, living with my nanny, it was supposed to be a new start."

She blinked back the tears in her eyes.

"Now I'm back to being alone. All my family are dead."

"Hey." Gently, Noah rested his hand on top of Cat's, forcing her to fix her gaze on him. "You have me now, and Evelyn, and Maria, and maybe even Jackson. We're here for you. We're your family now." His usual deep tone was now soft. If Cat weren't staring at his soothing smile, she wouldn't have recognised his voice.

A sad smile painted her lips.

"Thank you, Noah. That means so much to me. I've always wanted a big family."

The waitress approached the table, plates in her hands, and set them down in front of Cat and Noah. Though she wished she didn't have to, Cat pulled her hand from under Noah's and picked up her knife and fork. The sugary smell of syrup swirled beneath her nose, resulting in another loud growl from her stomach. She licked her lips and shoved the first bite into her mouth, her tastebuds exploding at the sweet taste.

Noah laughed.

"Well, if this is first date goes well, I think it's going well enough to plan for a second."

Cat arched her brow, a proud grin succeeding her melancholic smile.

"Is that so? I wasn't aware that this was a date, Detective," she teased. "Besides, if you wanted to go on a date, you'd have to ask me first, before you can call it as much."

"You got me there," Noah said.

His phone rang in his pocket, interrupting the tender moment. He inhaled the last of his pancakes and answered.

"Detective Thompson. Mhm. Yeah. Right. Let me know as soon as you learn anything. Thanks." The call ended. Cat leaned forward in her seat, curiosity itching at her.

"That was Evelyn. They couldn't get anything from the laptop or the envelope. No prints, no trace on the email. It seems our killer rerouted the email through multiple servers, so it'll take a while to get a trace on him."

Cat fell back in her seat, disappointment routing its way through her system.

"So, we have no leads on who or where the killer is. The only thing we have to go off now is the note my nanny left for me." She faced the window again and watched the rain race down the glass, blurring the images outside.

"We'll figure it out. Did you remember to bring the book with you?" Noah asked, drawing Cat's attention once again.

Cat dove her hand into her oversized bag and

pulled out two copies of the book.

"Here." She pushed her grandmother's copy across the table. "I know the story inside out. I don't know how the message relates to it."

Noah turned over the book and read the short description, nodding his head, raising his brow when he'd finished. He opened the book to the page where her grandmother had scrawled the riddle under the title, as if signing an autograph for a fan. He scanned the message, reading the last part aloud.

"The answer is hidden on page six..."

"I swear, that riddle sounds so familiar." Cat rustled the pages until she landed on page six and skimmed through the words. There was nothing there that she thought could lead to the answer.

"Turn to page six in that copy, Noah. Maybe she highlighted or underlined a specific line or phrase."

Noah did as Cat suggested and, unsurprisingly, she was right.

"Look here." He nudged the book to the middle of the table so that Cat could see too. "The word 'letter' is highlighted here and there are symbols along the corners of the margins. I can't tell what they are. Some sort of cipher, maybe?"

Cat reached for the book and turned it towards her. Her eyes lit up like a tree on Christmas.

"Yes, it is! My nanny taught me it when I was a child. She said every mystery writer must have their own cipher, so no one can discern your story before it's ready."

As she rummaged through her purse, she could feel Noah's intense stare lingering on her.

"I brought some of the most recent letters with me, but I don't know if the right one will be in here." She jerked her head from the bag, which startled Noah and sent him jolting back from the table.

"Can I borrow your pen?"

"Oh, yeah, sure." He tugged a pen from his handkerchief pocket; his brows furrowed in confusion as he held out the pen for Cat to take. She grabbed it from his hand, drew a napkin from the dispenser and began to doodle on the paper.

"I can't remember it completely, but I think I can remember enough for now to decipher this little snippet here in the corner." As she scribbled on the napkin, her tongue poked through her lips.

"That's cute, how you stick your tongue out like that when you're concentrating," Noah remarked, showcasing his crooked smile.

Cat blushed, withdrawing her tongue, and finished the final part of the message.

"This part here" – she pointed to the small cipher in the corner – "is a date: 15.3.1999."

Noah twirled the napkin around so he could see the writing.

"How did you figure that out?"

"Easy," Cat said. "Each symbol represents a letter of the alphabet. So, first, I had to translate that. For years, my nanny and I used this code to send messages to one another in the letters we didn't want anyone else to see – they were mainly concerning story concepts we had. Whenever we wanted to use it for dates and numbers, we'd take each letter of the alphabet and use wherever they came out of the 26 numbers in place of writing the numbers themselves. It's pretty easy once you get used to it."

She drew out the cipher on another napkin and linked them with the corresponding letters.

"It's called the pigpen – or masonic – cipher."

"That's so cool," Noah cooed.

"Isn't it!"

She went back to shuffling in her bag, searching for the few letters she had with her.

"Come to think of it, nanny had actually been mentioning my parents more and more in her letters, using that cipher, but she never mentioned needing to tell me anything about them specifically. I never thought much of it though. She usually did talk about them around my birthday – the date from the cipher," she explained. "They disappeared around the same time."

She withdrew her hand from her purse, clutching a stack of envelopes tied together by an elastic band.

"These are the last few letters she sent, starting from my birthday four months ago."

Noah took the bundle from Cat and parted the envelopes into two stacks.

"You take one half and I'll take the other?" he asked, meeting her gaze.

"Sure. If there's anything you can't decipher, let me know and I'll help." She slid the napkin across the table – something to assist him in his reading – and took the first envelope from her pile.

By the time she was on her third cup of coffee, morning had turned to afternoon. Four letters deep into her pile, she hadn't found anything that could be linked to the riddle her grandmother had left behind. It was another half hour before Noah jumped in excitement.

"Here, I think I found it! This one has the same date we found in the book." He passed the letter to Cat, who deciphered the code. No wonder she recognised the riddle.

"Catarina, your parents may be gone, but you still have your memories. They make you cry, but they'll also make you smile. They're formed in an instant but last for a lifetime. Those memories will always be close to your heart, especially the ones most important to you. That is where it is hidden."

Cat threw her hands in the air, drawing some unwanted attention. She leaned over the table so that only Noah could hear.

"Of course! It makes sense! A memory! She wrote it right here for me to find! The answer to the riddle is a memory!"

"Great!" Noah whispered. "What memory is it she wants you to remember, and what is hidden?"

The victorious smile on Cat's face faded.

"I-I don't know. I always assumed she meant it's where the love is hidden." She sat back against the booth and thought. She wracked her brain but came up with nothing.

"Do you think it has something to do with those passwords the killer wants?" Noah offered.

"I have no idea. Nanny never mentioned anything about passwords in her letters." She sat up, eyes widening. "She used to keep a diary, though. I could bet that if she wanted to tell me something about my parents or some passwords, she'd have it written in her diary."

Noah motioned for the waitress and asked for the bill.

"It's probably still somewhere in her house, then. We can head over there now and see if we can find anything," he noted as he signed the bill and smiled at the waitress.

Cat slid from the booth, clearing her envelopes off the table, stacking them back together and settling them into her bag. Her heart was beating rhapsodically in her chest. Joy sprinkled her emotions. She was so caught up in the excitement of finally having a lead, she didn't notice when she bumped into somebody on the way out until she heard a low grunt after their bodies had collided.

"I'm so sorry." She looked up at the man towering over her and recognised the male paramedic she seemed to be running into a lot lately. "Jackson, hi. I'm sorry, I should have been watching where I was going." She gripped one of her arms, closing herself off from the man.

"No problem," was all he said as he rubbed his abdomen.

"Cat! Noah! It's so good to run into y'all again!" Maria chimed in, pulling Cat into a dramatic hug. Cat smiled and greeted the energetic woman.

"You too!"

She prayed the paramedics were too hungry to talk. She yearned to get back to her grandmother's house and find that diary.

"You seem in a hurry, Cat. Where are you off to?" Maria asked.

"We're heading back to my nanny's place. We think there's something there that can help us catch her killer."

A sharp poke in her side had her turning to Noah, who gave her a disapproving look.

"What do you think is there that can help?" Jackson asked, his brow raised.

Cat fiddled with her thumbs, acutely aware of Noah's disapproving expression.

"Oh, we're not totally sure yet, but hopefully we'll find something," she rambled on.

Jackson just nodded his head.

"We should probably get going. I think we've overstayed our welcome." Noah inclined his head towards the waitress eyeballing them from behind the counter.

"Of course, enjoy your investigating!" Maria mused as she pushed Jackson further into the diner.

Outside, Cat turned on Noah.

"What was that look back there?" she asked, arms folded crossly over her chest.

"You can't offer information during an ongoing investigation to civilians – even if they're your friends," he answered, opening the door to the SUV. "When investigating murder, assume that you can't trust anyone."

He shut the door and didn't say another word.

CHAPTER ELEVEN

The house that was once a symbol of hope stood tall in the shadows, a blurry image through the rain-soaked glass of the window. Though Cat peered through the scattered raindrops, she didn't see the house as it now stood, covered in darkness. Instead, a little girl was scampering up the front steps of the garden, sun reflecting off her dark hair. A teddy bear dangled at her side, bouncing with every step the little girl took.

An older woman crouched by the front door, arms stretched out, bracing herself for the approaching impact of the little girl's body. The girl flung herself into the woman's arms, and she embraced her with a high-spirited laugh. When she pulled away, she stroked the little girl's hair, which was tied up in curly pigtails. She looked past her granddaughter to the two adults now making their own way up the steps, chuckling at their daughter's enthusiasm.

That was seventeen years ago. Two years before her parents had disappeared.

"Cat? Are you listening to me?"

Cat snapped out of her trance and shifted her attention back to Noah, who sat behind the wheel of the vehicle, now parked on the side of the street.

"Yes, sorry. I was just... remembering," she whispered, pushing the memory out of her mind.

Though it was a long time ago, her heart remembered it as if it had happened yesterday – the joy she'd felt when she saw her grandmother and the never-ending laughter sparked by her parents' infinite love for their eccentric daughter.

Noah's eyes softened at Cat's quiet demeanour. He knew by now that if she went quiet, something was wrong. He caressed her shoulder, offering her a smile, which quickly faded. His gaze fell to the floor.

"I know it's going to be hard going back in there. We can take a few minutes before we go in if you need to," he said.

Cat's breath hitched at the sadness in his voice. He really cared for her grandmother, that much was obvious.

"Thank you, Noah," she said, drawing his attention back up to her face. "You were there for my nanny for years when I wasn't able to be. She got lonely sometimes and I know she loved having you around. I can tell she meant a lot to you, and you her."

Noah's glassy eyes stared at her for a while. Though she wasn't completely comfortable with him yet, Cat knew she could trust Noah. Maybe someday she might even want something more than just friendship with the detective. She maintained eye contact, until Noah finally spoke up.

"Now it's my turn to thank you."

Cat smiled, happy to finally be of help to someone else in their time of need.

"Hopefully, we can find Margaret's journal in the house, and we can finally have something to go off."

Cat nodded her head, lifted her hand, and took Noah's in hers, gently squeezing his fingers.

"Let's go so," she said, and jumped out into the pouring rain.

***

The house that had once been a source of joy during Noah's childhood was now eerily silent, dark, and empty of all life. The front door creaked as it swung open.

Did it always do that? Noah couldn't remember.

The double doors seemed to tower over him, haunting his every step as he entered further into the house, rain dripping from the hem of his coat onto the cold wooden floorboards. Trying his best to ignore the sorrowful agony creeping up on him, he passed the doors and continued into the kitchen. According to his team, this was where the killer had entered the house.

He froze in the doorframe. Just last week, he and Margaret had been sitting at that island, plotting to bring home Margaret's granddaughter. Her excitement had danced around her with such grace at the idea of having Cat here with her. If only she'd gotten the chance to live that dream.

A single tear caressed his cheeks. He wiped it from his face and turned to the window above the sink. The killer had climbed through here, Noah was told, breaking a flowerpot as he entered.

It had been yellow and ugly, Noah remembered.

He laughed quietly to himself. He had fought with Margaret so many times about that flowerpot. It seemed so silly now. He had given it to her as a gift when he was a child – something he'd made in school – and she'd kept it all these years. That was just like her, to keep something so insubstantial for so many years. She really was family to him.

"Noah!" Cat called from the library, "I think I've found something! Get in here!"

Startled by the sudden sound of Cat's voice, Noah jumped where he stood by the window, kicking his foot against the cupboard door.

"Ow!" he shrieked, hopping on his leg and squeezing his foot, pain searing from his heel to his toes.

"Noah?" Cat called again.

"Coming," he grunted, setting his foot back on the floor.

The doors towered over him. He gulped. His stomach lurched at the sudden realisation that he'd have to enter that dreadful room.

***

A room that was once full of stories, happiness,

and love was now in ruins. Pages of books scattered the floor. A sole bookshelf lay overturned on the floor, crumpling books once cherished and loved by Cat's grandmother.

It took all her effort not to look at the blood-stained carpet mere feet from where she stood, a black journal glued to her fingers. Memories flooded her consciousness. Times from years past when she was a little girl dressed in a yellow gown. She vaguely remembered the room, though it looked so different now.

Cat forced those memories deep down into her subconscious, drowning them out for the time being. She must remain strong. It was what her grandmother would have wanted.

Crumpling pages alerted her to Noah's approaching footsteps.

"What did you find?"

Cat passed him the diary, never taking her eyes off the black dusty cover.

"Have you looked in it yet?" he asked, examining the spine of the book. She shook her head.

"No. I was a little distracted, if I'm completely honest."

Noah's gaze pivoted to where her grandmother's lifeless remains had lain only a few days ago. Cat held out her hand, her warm skin pressing against the back of Noah's knuckles, pulling his attention back to her, a sorrowful smile in her eyes. Noah smiled back at her briefly and shifted his attention back to the diary he held in his hands.

When he turned to the first page, a creased fragment of paper fluttered to the floor. Curious, Cat bent down to see what it was. When she got close enough, she noticed the familiar symbols on the paper, written in her grandmother's cursive handwriting.

"What is it?" Noah asked, peeking his head out from behind the diary.

"An address," Cat said, looking back up at him.

She stood up and handed the scrap of paper to him, taking the book back so that she could examine it herself. Lines of cipher painted the pages in black ink. Cat flipped through the pages. Five, ten, more than fifteen pages to translate.

Cat groaned.

I love you nanny, but you really know how to make things difficult, she thought.

"There's too much here to translate right now. I'll need to go back to the house and go through it page by page," she explained to Noah, who was scribbling in his notepad. "But there are a few words that—"

A thunderous buzzing sound drowned out Cat's voice. Noah muttered his apologies and reached into his pocket, wrestling to get his phone free. When he finally managed to retrieve it, he answered the call.

"Detective Thompson."

The corners of his lips twinged downward, and all emotion drained from his face.

"We currently have a victim displaying the same wounds and M.O. here in Athens. Looks like your killer followed us here, Detective."

Cat looked up from the ciphered pages and fixed her gaze on Noah's worried eyes. Suddenly, it felt as if she were on a rollercoaster; butterflies fluttered across her chest, uneasiness swimming in her stomach.

"We'll keep you in the loop throughout our investigation. Thank you, Detective."

He hung up.

"What was that about?" Cat asked, a tangle of scenarios invading her brain.

"The autopsy on your uncle has been completed. The killer used the same M.O. on Neil Gallagher as was used on Margaret."

Cat gasped, though she wasn't sure why. It made sense when she thought about it. Her uncle had been murdered and, nearly a day later, somebody had killed her grandmother. There would have been plenty of time for the killer to return to America and drive to her grandmother's house.

"Evelyn and the team are investigating their end – the laptop and the decoy." He brushed a finger along Cat's cheek, sending a chilling sensation through her skin. "We need to keep looking too. Starting with this diary."

"But if the same person really did kill my uncle and my nanny, then it's likely that I'm next," she mumbled.

Noah sucked in a deep breath.

"There's something I need to tell you, but not here. We have to go back to the precinct."

Noah leaned against the chair, pressing all his weight into his hands, relieving his knee of pain from standing on it all day. It seemed to be giving him more and more trouble these days.

"Sit rep," his Chief of Police, Blake Richardson, ordered. He was a tall man – much taller than Noah. Probably a little over six feet tall, Noah reckoned. His athletic build almost put Noah's to shame, but what else could he expect from an old Navy Seal. As far as Noah had ever witnessed, he was well trained and deadly with his weapons.

"We found this diary in Margaret O'Donnell's home. It's written in code, but Cat here can translate it for us." Blake grunted in acknowledgement. "I also received a phone call from the detective back in Ireland. The medical examiner there concluded that Neil Gallagher was murdered in the same fashion as our vic," Noah concluded.

Blake stood behind his desk chair, his arms crossed.

"We must assume that Catarina here is the next target. I'll arrange for a cruiser to be positioned outside your house all hours of the day. Margaret was one of our own. God knows she trailed us enough for her books. We won't let anything happen to her granddaughter."

Noah sighed in relief, thankful his friend saw what the necessary actions were to keep Cat safe from the killer.

Blake turned his attention to Evelyn, who stood in the shadows by the doorway.

"Detective Joy, any progress tracking that email?"

She stepped forward. Light illuminated her pale skin; dark bags lined her tired eyes.

"Yessir. Our tech team believe we should have the location of where the email originated from by tomorrow evening at the latest."

"Very good," Blake said, and faced the last remaining person in the room. "Miss Gallagher, if there is anything you need, let me know. I'll do the best I can to help you in any way possible. All you have to do is ask."

"Thank you, Mr. Richardson, sir."

"Please, call me Blake." He held out his hand. Cat stared at it for a moment. Noah felt the urge to jump between his Chief and Cat – to protect her. He took a step forward, when Cat cautiously extended her own arm and grasped Blake's hand, shaking it once and quickly stepping backwards.

Pride forced a smile onto Noah's face.

"I'd like to request permission to bring in some reinforcements," Noah addressed Blake, now standing tall with his hands behind his back. Blake arched his eyebrow.

"Who do you need?"

"Oliver Campbell, Benjamin Myers, and Wyatt Gray."

The room remained silent for a fraction of a moment.

"Okay. Call them if you need them. But remember, this is official police business.

Everything has to be done by the book."

Noah bobbed his head in agreement and thanked the Chief.

"How long will it take to find out who that address belongs to?" he asked Evelyn.

"A couple hours, maybe. The staff are backlogged. Too many crimes, not enough officers," she answered, irritation lacing her voice.

"I have a friend who can get it done faster," Blake chimed in. "Give me ten minutes."

And he walked from the room.

Cat twirled around to Noah, her stare gluing him to the floor.

"You can't just tell me that there's something I need to know, drag me here and then not tell me!" she exclaimed. There was a hint of a snarl in her voice. Noah made a mental note to never get on her bad side again.

"I'm sorry sweetheart, we had to update Blake before we could do anything else."

She tapped her foot on the floor impatiently. If he squinted hard enough, maybe he'd be able to see steam floating from her ears. Evelyn watched them, a humorous glint in her eyes. Noah shot her a dirty look, and she raised her hands in surrender. Noah could tell it was taking her a great effort to keep herself from laughing at his current situation.

"Well?" Cat demanded, her arms folded over her chest.

"Okay, I surrender."

He sighed. He knew that this would upset

Cat, but if he didn't tell her, she could be in even more danger.

"When we found the receptionist in your hotel room... there was a second message on the bathroom mirror."

Cat's arms fell to her sides. Noah took a deep breath and closed his eyes.

"It said you were next."

He opened his eyes to find Cat falling into one of the chairs in front of the desk.

***

"It's all my fault. Everything is my fault," Cat cried hysterically into her hands. Tears rolled off her cheeks by the dozen. Her chest heaved, trying to force her to take a breath – to calm down – but she couldn't. Her family had died because of her. Wherever she went, death seemed to follow. The killer had already threatened Noah. What if he came after anyone else – Evelyn, Maria, even Jackson had managed to make her feel welcome, even if it were in as few words as possible. She couldn't let anyone else die because of her.

"Hey now." Evelyn was at her side in seconds, holding her in her arms, talking in a hushed tone. "It's not your fault, Cat. This person is a madman. He's doing this not because of you, but because of something he wants. And we don't even know exactly what that is yet."

She looked past Cat to Noah, who crouched down on the other side of the chair.

"If it hadn't been Margaret, it would have

been you, and Margaret wouldn't have wanted that." He spoke so softly, so soothingly, Cat almost felt herself relax. Involuntarily, she breathed in until her lungs could hold no more air, and she sighed, sniffing her disgustingly wet nose. Evelyn handed her a packet of Kleenex, and she got to work on wiping the tears from her face. Though stragglers remained to make their way down her cheeks after she had finished, Cat leaned back against the chair.

"I miss her. I miss her so much."

The tears started again.

"I know sweetheart. I do too," Noah said, pulling her into his shoulder.

Cat wrapped her arms around his neck and suppressed the oncoming sobs. She sniffled, trying not to get snot on Noah's clean shirt.

"I had only just said hello. I never got to say goodbye."

She closed her eyes and tried to breathe. Noah's hand stroked her hair, turning her short, struggling breaths into steady, even ones.

"I know. I know, sweetheart."

They sat there for several minutes, until Cat's heartbeat returned to a normal pace, and she could breathe with ease. Her tired eyes struggled to stay open. Blake stormed back into the room, only stopping when he noticed Cat enveloped in Noah's embrace. He cleared his throat, drawing their attention.

Cat pulled herself from Noah's arms and wiped her cheeks, which were now flushed pink from embarrassment. Evelyn flashed her a pretty smile and winked.

"What is it, Chief?" she asked, drawing the man's attention from Cat's miserable state. Relief flooded Cat when his gaze left her. She was grateful for Evelyn's friendship.

"The address. It belongs to a Senator Mills."

His eyes fell back on Cat.

"We have a third victim."

***

Noah punched a number into his phone as he pulled into his driveway.

"Pack enough for a few days," he told Cat. "We don't know how long it'll take to get the information we need."

Cat opened her door and disappeared into the house just as a voice came over the phone.

"Hello?"

"Oliver, it's me."

Oliver's groggy voice echoed across the cabin of the SUV.

"What's up, Captain? It's 2.30 in the morning."

"I need you and the guys to meet me in Nashville by tomorrow evening. I'm investigating a case. Some madman is killing off the family of a girl I, er... care for."

The shuffling of sheets reverberated through the phone.

"We'll be there. Anything for you, brother."

"Thanks man. I'll text you the address. Meet us there and I'll give you the sit rep tomorrow."

The call ended.

Noah leaned back in his seat, relishing in the solace provided by his former Ranger unit coming to his aid. Cat stepped up into the SUV, duffel bag in her hand.

"Do you not have to pack?" she yawned.

Noah shook his head and pointed to his go bag resting on the back seat.

"I always have one ready, just in case."

He reversed from the garden and pulled onto the road.

"Where exactly are we going, by the way? We rushed from the precinct so fast I didn't have time to catch on to what was happening," Cat pressed.

Wherever they were going, Noah was definitely in a hurry to get there. Buildings zoomed by in a blur as the SUV raced down the road.

"Where are we going, Noah?"

He glanced at her tired expression.

"Nashville, Tennessee."

CHAPTER TWELVE

Illuminated lights cast over the shadowed roads. Stars shimmered in the sky above, providing even more light for Noah as he zoomed past buildings and trees. Cat rested her head against the window, her eyes closed, a sweet smile on her lips. Noah smiled to himself, happy that she'd managed to get some rest through the night.

It was 4.30 a.m. They'd only been driving two hours and already Noah could feel the last of the caffeine leaving his system. He envied Cat's ability to sleep.

"What are you staring at," Cat mumbled as she raised her head from its resting position and turned to face Noah. Dark lines marked the skin under her eyes.

"I uhh–"

Noah paused in his answer. Though it was dark, he could still make out the frizzy curls on the right side of her head. He shoved a hefty laugh back down his throat, but not before a small chuckle escaped his lips. Cat's eyes turned to slits as she glared at him. Quickly, he returned his gaze to the road ahead, avoiding her icy cat-like glare.

He cleared his throat.

"I wasn't staring at anything."

He paused, a grin tweaking the corners of his lips upward.

"Nice hair, by the way."

"What?" Cat lifted her hands to her head and patted at her hair. "Oh, for feck sake." She combed her fingers through her matted hair, doing her best to get rid of the frizz. "Sometimes I'd just love to take some scissors to me hair."

Noah furrowed his eyebrows.

"That's some Irish accent," he mused.

Turning onto a smaller road surrounded by trees, he checked his mirrors, making sure they weren't being tailed. As far as he could see, there were no other cars behind him.

"Yeah," Cat yawned, "my accent tends to be stronger when I'm tired or annoyed. You should probably get used to hearing me call people eejits and saying feck a lot. I'll also say that's grand and what's the craic." She sat back in the seat, giving up on trying to fix her tangled curls. "How much longer until we get to Nashville?"

Noah glanced at the clock next to the speedometer.

"About another three hours."

Cat groaned, wiping her face with the palms of her hands.

"I suppose I should make use of the time and go through this diary so."

She reached into her handbag, pulled out the black book and set it on her lap.

***

Exhaustion clung to Cat as if its life depended on it. The roads were empty. She squinted to make out the writing on the pages. Darkness embraced the cabin of the SUV.

"Use the flashlight on your phone if you need to," Noah said, keeping his eyes on the road ahead.

Cat tugged her phone from her jeans pocket and switched on the flashlight function. For a moment, the light blinded her vision, until it finally adjusted to the new setting. She hovered the light over the first page of the journal and began to read.

Ten minutes later, Cat broke the silence as she deciphered the fifth page. The phone fell to the floor. She covered her mouth with her hand, a gasp slipping past her lips.

"What? What is it?" Noah asked, worry lacing its way through his words.

He cast a concerned look her way, quickly shifting his focus back to the road. The SUV swerved to the side, barely missing a rogue deer by mere inches. The book slid to the floor, just out of reach as the car veered back onto the road. Her arms stretched out, Cat leaned forward, but she still could not reach. Without a word, she unbuckled her seatbelt.

"What are you doing, Cat? Put your seatbelt back on!" Noah demanded.

"I've... almost... got it."

Without warning, the car screeched to a stop. Cat lurched forward, hands above her head, ready to break the impact of the dashboard.

But it never came.

Fingers tightened around her arm and pulled her back. Eyes closed; her head bashed into the soft headrest behind her.

"I told you to put your seatbelt back on! What on earth were you doing!" Noah cried, his grip tightening.

"You're hurting me," Cat mumbled, horror in her eyes. Noah released his clasp on her upper arm.

"Sorry," he muttered. "You scared the crap out of me." A coat of fear was embedded in his eyes. His voice now husky, he whispered, "You could have been killed."

"Me? You scared the crap out of me!" Cat exclaimed, massaging her tender arm. "Why did you stop like that anyway?"

Noah inclined his head towards the front of the car.

"Take a look."

Cat's eyes widened in shock and awe at the three animals disappearing into the trees on the other side of the road.

"Deer?" she asked.

Noah nodded his head.

"White-tailed deer. Very common in Tennessee. Now, buckle your seatbelt before I continue on driving."

Cat leaned forward in her seat for the final time and grabbed the book. Sitting back, she secured her seatbelt and faced Noah.

"Happy?" she asked, a sarcastic tone in her

voice.

"Yes." He continued driving down the long road. "What did you read in that book that surprised you?"

Cat returned to the page she had been on and began to read.

"It's taken some time, but I've finally found it – the reason why David and Emily were on that dreaded plane to America. After all these years, I thought it was for a business trip. I was wrong. It wasn't a business trip at all..."

Her voice trailed off. Memories spun a web in her mind. Memories of the day her parents left for America. She'd been only five years old. She didn't remember much from that day, but she did remember how her parents had acted. It had been complete and utter chaos. Her parents had been frantic; buzzing around the house trying to get their affairs in order. Cat had always thought it weird for people to leave it so late in the evening to go on a business trip.

But if it wasn't a business trip, what was it...?

Her thoughts landed on the memory of that night, when her mother had given her the locket. She had said something as she clasped the necklace around Cat's neck. But what was it?

She replayed the memory time after time in her head, urging her mind to remember that one last thing her mother had told her. She squeezed her eyes shut, took a deep breath in, and allowed all her memories to flood her mind – her parents, the picnics under the tree, everything.

Her eyes shot open.

When we come home, you're going to have a big brother, Catarina.

Oh. My. God.

"I remember. I remember what my mam told me before they left."

She twisted in her seat so that her entire body faced Noah. Though he couldn't turn to face her, Cat noted the intrigued look on her friend's face.

"A kid."

"A what?"

"They were flying to America to get a kid. That's all I can remember. My mam told me the night they left that when they returned, I'd have a big brother."

"Wow..."

Cat stared out the window into the looming darkness, wondering what had really happened to her parents. And what had become of the boy who was going to be her brother?

***

"What else does the book say?" Noah asked. He didn't know what to think, what information to process first. What *did* happen to the kid? Were the Gallagher's deaths really an accident, or something more? With each answer they learned, even more questions were revealed.

The rustling of pages caught his attention as Cat scanned through the book. He waited patiently for her to answer his question.

"Here!" Cat smacked her finger against one of the pages as she cried out. "It says here that their plane was scheduled to land in Nashville National Airport! But wait..."

She went quiet.

More rustling of pages. Then, "There's nothing else. That was the last entry," Cat announced half-heartedly. She slumped in her seat. Out of the corner of his eye, Noah watched as she closed her eyes and began to sob.

Noah lifted his right hand from the steering wheel and set it on Cat's leg.

"We'll figure it all out, sweetheart, I promise."

He kept his hand there, not daring to move it until he knew that the girl sitting next to him would be alright.

The warmth of skin against his knuckles willed him to shift his attention to her hand, softly sitting on top of his own, if only for a moment. Her glassy eyes smiled at him, entrancing him further. With a smile, Noah directed his attention on the road ahead, continuing their adventure into the unknown.

***

Trees spread along the street across from the house, concealing His every move. A single police cruiser sat next to the path. The streets were empty. Quietly, He snuck through the trees and bushes, careful to remain hidden from the officer seated next to the open door. The air reeked of tobacco. He hissed at the putrid scent. The officer stood leaning against the heavy metal. He twisted his head and squinted into the dark.

"Who's there?" he called out, grabbing a black cylindrical object from his belt.

He retreated into the thickest of bushes, ensuring He made enough sound to draw the officer's attention. A flicker of light shone through the trees. The officer advanced into the dark, away from the safety of his car – away from the safety of the public.

"APD, show yourself!"

He was so close. Just a few more steps...

When he was close enough, and far enough away from the street, He plunged at the officer, scalpel gripped in His hand, ready to slice. They fell to the ground, rolling in the dirt.

"No!" the officer yelled, clawing at His face with one hand as he tried to push Him off with the other. It was no use, though. He was too strong for him.

Straddling the officer, He pulled back His arm, ready to deliver the killing blow. He pinned the officer's arm to the ground and struck.

Blood spurted from the officer's neck, soaking His skin and His clothes. Not that it mattered. There was nobody around to see a blood-soaked man walking about the streets of the suburbs this late at night, anyway.

He hoisted Himself off the lifeless remains, stepped over the dead officer, and strolled back towards the house, whistling to Himself as He walked. When He reached the street, the cruiser remained abandoned by the curb. It wouldn't be too long before darkness turned to light, and somebody noticed the missing officer.

Time was ticking.

He crossed the road and hopped up the steps to the front door of Detective Noah Thompson's humble abode. He hunkered down on one knee and pulled two pins from His trouser pocket. Carefully, He twisted one pin and inserted the second, slowly moving each one until He heard the satisfying *click* of the lock. The door swung open, and He was greeted with an empty house. He took the first step into the house and waited. An alarm greeted Him.

Of course the detective had an alarm.

Time was certainly ticking now.

He scanned the layout of the house. A living room, a kitchen, and a bathroom. If He were the detective, He'd keep the files somewhere safe, but where? He turned and hurried into the living room. He didn't have much time. He pulled the cushions from the sofa, books from the coffee table, picture frames from the walls.

One painting hung just out of place on the wall behind the sofa. He cocked His head to the side. It was crooked. With ease, He jumped onto the sofa and heaved the painting from the wall, disposing of it onto the floor. A grin plastered across His face, he examined the security pad of the old safe hidden within the wall.

A pin pad.

He needed the four-digit pin.

Sirens sang in the distance, pressuring Him to hurry. He rushed to the pantry, grabbed a jar of flour, and hopped back onto the sofa. With a handful of flour resting on His palm, He forced the air from His mouth, showering the pin pad with the powdery substance. Fingerprints revealed themselves on four of the buttons.

The sirens grew louder.

Now for the tricky part.

He scoured His brain for information – anything that He'd learned in His research of the detective that would help Him crack the code. Instantly, He knew what it could be.

Six. Three. Ninety-nine.

His gloved fingers swept over the keys. The door *clicked* and swung open.

He'd found the files.

He grabbed the pile of files from the safe and leapt from the sofa. Flashing lights lit up the night sky outside the window.

He had run out of time.

Cops swarmed the front of the house and the abandoned cruiser outside. In one swift movement, He turned from the window and hurried towards the back door. If He could make it out before they breached the threshold, He had a chance at escaping.

As He reached the back door, someone barged through the front entrance and cocked their gun at the back of His head. He froze, His hand on the door handle.

"Put your hands behind your head and turn around!" the cop yelled. He stood at the further end of the hall.

He still had a chance.

Ducking, He pulled on the handle of the door and ran out into the woods.

***

The soft mattress embraced Noah's aching body. His muscles tense from hours of driving had finally begun to relax. He let out a sigh of relief, closing his tired eyes and relishing the comfort of the scratchy linen sheets. A soft chuckle reverberated throughout the room.

"Comfy?" Cat asked once she had finished laughing.

"As much as one can be on a motel bed," Noah answered. "But I'm tired and sore, so it'll do."

"Well..." Cat dropped her go bag onto the twin bed. "Considering this was the last available room, the perception of motel beds being notoriously uncomfortable doesn't seem to hold up, does it?"

Noah's eyelids flipped open, and a cocky smile crossed his face.

"Affairs, sweetheart. One doesn't need to sleep in the bed in order to rent the room."

Heat coursed through Cat's cheeks, causing them to flush a bright shade of pink.

"I see," she muttered.

Noah watched her as she glanced back at him, only to turn away again when she saw his mischievous grin and the twinkle in his eyes. He pushed himself from the mattress, tugging his shirt back down to his waistline. It had risen up when he'd stretched his arms above his head on the mattress. Whoops.

"The guys should be here in a few hours. I'll head out and grab us some breakfast. Then we should rest so that we're ready to bring my team up to date on the investigation."

Cat nodded her agreement and pulled clean clothes from her bag as Noah stifled a yawn and rubbed his tired eyes, dragged himself off the bed and made for the door.

"I won't be long," Noah called back to her as he shut the door behind him.

***

Cat pulled the curtains closed, blocking the view into the room. The last thing they needed was the wrong person to find her here, alone. Just as she stepped into the old, rusting shower, a buzzing noise sounded from the bedroom. Wrapping a towel around herself, she hurried into the room to find Noah's ringing phone on the crumpled sheets.

She picked up the phone and answered the call.

"Hello?"

"Cat, is that you?" Evelyn asked on the other side of the call.

"Yeah, sorry, Noah just went out to get breakfast. Looks like he forgot his phone. Do you want me to take a message?"

Silence.

"You still there?"

Butterflies tickled Cat's stomach. Something didn't seem right.

Finally, "No, it's alright, thanks. Have him call me when he gets back."

"Grand," Cat responded, and the call ended.

What was that about? Had something happened?

***

Twenty minutes later, Noah returned to the motel, a bag of bagels and two bottles of water in his hands. He unlocked the door and entered the room, only to find it empty.

"Cat? Cat are you here?" he called.

No answer.

Throwing the bagels and water on the small table, he rushed about the small room. There didn't seem to be any sign of a struggle and water droplets were sprinkled across the shower wall.

Where was she?

His chest pounded; worry overpowered his every thought. Not again. He couldn't lose another person. Hadn't he already lost enough? He scanned the room. Her go bag was still on her bed, unzipped, clothes scattered everywhere. He closed in on the bag, rooting through it to find any clue of where she could have gone, when the door jerked open.

His hand flung to his holster and he drew his weapon, switched the safety off and aimed at the intruder. A girl faced him, terror in her eyes. A bucket fell from her arms, sending ice shooting across the floor, some shattering on impact.

Noah holstered his weapon as quickly as he'd

drawn it.

"Cat, I'm so sorry. I didn't mean to scare you. I couldn't find you and then–"

"It's grand, Noah." She bent down to pick up the ice scattered across the floor. "I shouldn't have left. I'm sorry. I just thought it'd be nice to have some ice in our drinks. It's hotter here than it is back in Athens."

Relieved that she was okay, Noah pulled her into his arms, letting go after a few moments to help her pick up the shards of ice.

"Oh, by the way," Cat spoke up, "Evelyn called. She has news, but she wouldn't tell me what it was. She said to call her back when you returned."

Noah searched his pockets for his phone, only now realising that he'd left it behind when he'd gone out for their breakfast.

"Thanks, I'll call her now."

Taking the phone from Cat's open palm, Noah pressed the speed dial. Evelyn answered on the second ring.

"Noah. Something's happened. It's bad."

Noah excused himself from the room and walked out into the car park.

"Tell me."

"The officer stationed outside your house last night was found dead. Murdered. And someone broke into your house. All the case files are gone, Noah."

Noah's heart raced. Though the thought of somebody killing a fellow officer and breaking into his home infuriated him, he was relieved that

Cat wasn't there when it happened.

"And Noah," Evelyn continued, "he was killed the same way as Margaret O'Donnell and Neil Gallagher."

Bile slithered up Noah's throat.

He'd killed. Again.

"Thanks for telling me, Lyn. We've arrived in Nashville. My team arrives tonight. I'll keep Cat safe if it's the last thing I do."

If he had to take a bullet to save Catarina Gallagher's life, he'd gladly do it. No one else was going to die on his watch.

"There's one more thing."

Noah pressed the phone to his ear, anticipation weighing down on him.

"We managed to trace the IP address of the email sent to the actor. It came from Maria Gonzalez's home computer. We have her in custody now, but Noah, every time someone's described the perp, they've said 'he'."

"Question her. See if she knows anything. There are no such things as coincidences," Noah warned.

"I know. Be careful, Noah."

"Don't worry about me. I'll let you know when we have more answers."

He pressed the *end call* button and walked back into the motel room, massaging the back of his neck, to find Cat stuffing her face with bagels. Resembling a chipmunk, she asked, "What's wrong?"

Noah sat next to her and pulled out a bagel for himself.

"There's been another murder. An officer this time. And the tech team traced the email to Maria's home computer."

CHAPTER THIRTEEN

A single knock on the door drew Cat's attention from the novel in her hands. The sun was hanging in the sky, and hunger struck her like a baseball bat hitting a home run. Noah pushed himself from the bed next to Cat's and peered through the miniscule parting in the dark curtains.

"The guys are here," was all he said as he turned the lock on the door.

Cat closed her book and laid it down on the rumpled sheets beside her.

Three large men entered the room, each taller than the last. All three men were ruggedly handsome – if you liked broad shoulders and arm muscles. They'd had to have been fit though, Cat supposed, since they'd all been Rangers in the military. They all carried black duffel bags like Noah's. Once they were in the room and the door was closed, all their eyes fell on Cat.

Feeling their gazes on her should have given her the urge to cocoon herself under the duvet and hide from these strangers, but she didn't feel the need to hide.

Weird.

Her stomach knotted at all the attention

directed her way, and her heartbeat quickened, but somehow, she felt safe. She wasn't sure why. She looked over at Noah, who stood by the closed door, watching her reaction to the intruders in the room.

"Hey darlin'," one of the men spoke up, a strong southern drawl in his words. "Wyatt Gray. It's a pleasure to meet you."

He didn't hold out his hand, but instead nodded his head at Cat, a flirty grin on his lips. Cat wondered how much Noah had told these guys about her.

"Oliver Campbell, at your service," the second introduced himself. His kind hazel eyes contrasted with his intimidating stance.

"And I'm Benjamin Myers, but you can call me Benji," the last of them said with a wink.

A hint of a smile twitched at Cat's lips.

"Benji here is our sniper. He can hit any target he sets his sights on." Noah clapped the man on his back.

Oliver stepped forward and pulled Noah into a bear hug. "Oliver's our medic. I've never trusted another man with my life as much as I have old Oli here."

"Watch it, Cap, I'm the same age as you. Better looking too."

Laughing, Noah gripped Wyatt's hand and shook it vigorously. "And if you ever want anything blown up, Wyatt here is your guy. I've never met someone who likes a good detonation more."

Cat's eyes beamed at Noah's happiness. She

had never seen him so relaxed. Noah's demeanor changed, however, causing her smile to suddenly fade.

"There's one more person we can't forget," Noah muttered. All the eyes in the room fell to the ground. There was a moment of silence. Finally, Benjamin spoke up.

"Lance Peters – our spotter. He uh... he never made it home from our final mission."

Cat cupped her hands around her mouth.

"I'm so sorry, I didn't know," she said.

"It's okay, I never told you. It was my fault." Noah lifted his gaze from the floor, a glassiness enhancing the light blue hue of his eyes. "He got caught in the crossfire because I turned my back to him."

"Hey now, it wasn't your fault. You were just doing your job," Oliver chimed in. "Besides, maybe we have a new spotter now." His eyes flicked to Cat.

"I'll let her spot me any day," Wyatt said, mischief in his smile.

"You're not even a sniper, doucheface," Benjamin laughed.

"Okay, okay. That's enough flirting from the three of you." Noah moved in place beside Cat's bed, seemingly facing off against the three men.

"It isn't our fault you didn't tell us how gorgeous this little darlin' here is, Cap. You didn't give us time to prepare," Wyatt remarked. The other two men shrugged in agreement. Noah directed his icy glare at each of them in turn.

"It's alright, Noah."

Cat settled her hand on Noah's arm, pulling his attention to her. She smiled and climbed from the bed.

"It's nice to meet you all." She grinned at the men who now stood so close to her. She sucked in a deep breath, slowly releasing it as she stepped in front of Noah's friends and extended her hand.

One by one, she shook each man's hand. To everyone's surprise – especially her own – she didn't cower once, nor did she feel the urge to run away. Noah came up behind her and wrapped his arm around her. At that moment, Cat's stomach rumbled so loudly, she was sure she could almost be cast as Chewbacca in the next Star Wars film.

Boisterous laughter erupted around the room.

"Sounds like we need to feed this little lady," Oliver chuckled, a hard city accent revealing itself. Cat couldn't place it exactly, though. She wasn't well enough acquainted with the different accents yet.

"Yes, please." She purred at the thought of food. She really wanted to try out those American cheeseburgers and fries everyone was always talking about.

"We'll just throw our stuff in our room and meet y'all in the parking lot," Benjamin proposed.

"You got a room?" Noah asked, puzzled. "Just this morning, the place was fully booked."

"Oh yeah. It took a little convincing, if you know what I mean, but we got one alright. Meet you outside in ten."

And they left.

Cat waited a few moments to see if Noah would remove his arm from her waist.

"Someone's protective," she teased when he didn't pull away.

She turned in Noah's arms and met his gaze. Their eyes – only inches apart – locked on one another. His sweet, gentle eyes stared back at her. He pulled her in closer.

"I promised myself I wouldn't let anything happen to you. I trust my men, but sometimes they come on a little too strong," he whispered.

Cat's eyes dropped to his parting lips. She watched as the words poured from his mouth, then she flicked her gaze back up.

"I feel safe when I'm with you," she responded.

He wrapped his other arm around her waist and rested his hands on the small of her back, holding her in place. She could have moved away from him if she wanted to, but she found that she didn't. Her heart fluttered in her chest. She pressed her body closer to Noah's, leaving no open space between them, and wrapped her arms around his neck.

"Cat," Noah whispered softly in her ear.

"It's okay. I'm okay," she said.

Slowly, she leaned in, closing her eyes. For the first time since she was a child, she felt completely safe. Nothing could harm her as long as Noah Thompson was by her side.

A soft knock sounded against the door, startling Cat. She pulled back, her gaze now locked on the door handle, which was jiggling up and down as someone attempted to open the door. Noah tiptoed across the room to the window and peered through the curtains. His hand hovering over his holster, he opened the door.

"Well hell-oh, um, wrong room, sorry!"

A young lady, probably not much older than Cat herself, scurried down the path in nothing but heels and a coat. Cat released the shaky breath she had been holding in and bent down to pick up her trainers. Noah rolled his eyes as he shut the door.

"The guys are probably waiting for us. We should head out," Cat announced.

"Oh, yeah sure. Let's go."

Noah picked up his jacket from the bedside chair and threw it over his shoulders. He opened the door for Cat and followed her out into the afternoon heat.

***

After double checking that the door was secure, Noah turned and headed over to the small group gathered in the car park. Thoughts rushed through his mind.

Had he really been about to kiss Cat?

What was that fluttering feeling in his stomach?

"Ah! There he is!" Oliver jogged over to Noah, pulling him back to reality. Concern etched across his face at Noah's reddened cheeks. "Is something wrong, Cap?"

Noah just shook his head as the pair walked through the car park a few feet behind Cat and the rest of his team, unable to think of anything to say. Her hair danced in the mild breeze as she skipped alongside Wyatt and Benjamin, engaging them in conversation. A hopeless sense of pride coursed through Noah's veins. Though he was happy that she was finally beginning to relax around other men, he couldn't help but feel a spark of jealousy rising from within.

Cat twirled around as she walked and called back to Noah and Oliver.

"Hurry up, slow pokes! I'm starving!"

She giggled and spun back around just in time to face the giant SUV in front of her.

"No – I don't know. At least I don't think so," Noah blubbered, finally answering his friend's question as he watched Wyatt open the back door of the SUV for Cat, who smiled her pretty smile back at him and climbed into her seat. A hint of green sparkled in Noah's eyes. He stopped a few feet from the others, Oliver drawing to a stop beside him.

"We almost kissed, back in the room. Me and Cat. But some woman knocked on the door and interrupted the moment. Now I don't know what to do or what to say to her. I don't know how she feels, or if she even feels anything," he ranted.

"Whoa, whoa, Cap. Take a breath." Oliver raised his hands, sucking in a deep breath, and slowly lowered them as he eased the air out through his open mouth. Noah copied the motion.

"First of all, man, have you ever even been with a girl before? You're seriously freaking out! Second, look at her. She obviously likes you. We could see it the moment we entered the room back there just from how she was looking at you. Then she didn't push you away when you decided to be a macho man and claim your territory. Given her history, that's pretty big." They picked up their stride again. "You'll never live that down by the way," he laughed. "But don't you worry, we'll be here for her when you mess up."

He flashed a cheeky grin at Noah and slid into the passenger seat. Noah climbed into the back and sat himself next to Cat, a shy smile colouring his rosy cheeks. Wyatt and Benjamin flashed him their cocky grins when they noticed his odd behaviour.

"Where to, darlin'?" Wyatt turned in his seat to face the team, his eyes landing on Cat. Noah offered a silent glare at his friend, whose lips twitched into a smirk.

"Anywhere with chicken and burgers. I'm dying for a cheeseburger," Cat chirped. Her stomach growled again, setting off a low rumble of chuckles throughout the SUV.

***

Cat eyed the menu resting in her hands. Her stomach gurgled, begging to be fed. She couldn't hold back much longer. She needed food, fast. She examined the restaurant with interest. A bar stood against the back wall. Tables and chairs filled the small space, lights irradiating the darkened room. A few people were scattered throughout the restaurant, but it wasn't full. Cat groaned, wondering what was taking the waiter so long.

"I can't choose between the hot chicken tenders or the Sonoran burger..."

She eyed each of the men sitting at her table, hoping at least one of them would catch the hint. With almost too much effort, Wyatt, Benji and Oliver scoured their own menus, not daring to look up.

Noah dropped his menu on the wooden table.

"You get the burger and I'll get the chicken. We can share," he said, avoiding eye contact.

"My hero!" Cat cooed, a smile almost bigger than her face covering her cheeks.

The earlier events of the evening lingered in her thoughts. Their lips had been so close – closer than anyone had ever gotten to her before. She reached across the table and sat her hand over Noah's, drawing his gaze to hers. He cupped her hand in his own, his eyes twinkling in the colourful lights surrounding the room. His expression was a cross between worry and curiosity. His brows furrowed slightly, his head tilted at an angle, but his eyes remained wide open, asking a silent question.

"I'm okay," Cat whispered, squeezing the palms of his hand. She stretched her legs under the table and brushed against a boot in front of her.

Wyatt glanced up from his menu.

"Eh darlin', that's my leg."

Cat slid down in her chair and used her menu to conceal her blushing cheeks.

"Sorry," she mumbled from behind the laminated card.

A brush against her leg drew her attention away from her humiliation. Another brush had her peeking out at Noah from behind the menu. He smiled at her from across the table and winked.

"Ready to order?"

Cat started in her seat. She didn't even notice the waiter come over to their table. The waiter eyed her, waiting for an answer.

"Yes, please," Noah answered for her.

As each person at the table ordered their meal, Cat kept her gaze focused on Noah, watching him interact with his friends, noticing how every once in a while, he'd flick his eyes sideways at her and quickly look away. When the food finally came twenty minutes later, Cat almost forgot that she was supposed to be sharing her burger with Noah. She raised the burger to her lips, ready for her first glorious mouthful when he reminded her.

"Sorry," she laughed, digging her knife and fork into the bread and meat, slicing it into two pieces. She handed half of the burger over to Noah, who swapped it for some chicken.

"So, Cat, what's brought you to America?" Benji asked, amused by the amount of food she could fit into her mouth at once.

His grin, however, quickly faded from his face

when Cat began to choke on her burger, coughing uncontrollably. Oliver pushed himself from the table and rushed to her side as the coughing came to an end. Her face void of colour, he held up a drink to her lips and urged her to swallow the cool liquid.

Through teary eyes, Cat noticed Noah whispering aggressively to the two men still seated at the table. She passed the cup back to Oliver and thanked him while he rubbed her back. As he seated himself once more, Benjamin spoke up.

"Oh man, I'm so sorry, Cat. I didn't know. If I had, I wouldn't have asked."

Napkin in hand, Cat wiped the streaming tears from under her eyes.

"It's okay, Benji, don't worry about it. You'd have found out about it eventually, anyway."

"Is this why we're here?" Wyatt piped in, shoving a forkful of mac n' cheese into his mouth.

Noah's chest expanded as he took a deep, calming breath.

"Yes, it is." He cleared his throat, glancing at Cat for a brief moment then back to his friends. "Do you want to explain it, Cat, or will I?"

There was a moment of silence, and then, "It should be me. I have to face my own past eventually."

Noah nodded in agreement.

All eyes fell on Cat. For several moments, she froze, unable to bring the words past her lips. She closed her eyes and clutched her locket, but she didn't count to four. After a second, her eyes flicked open and she began retelling her tale – every single detail, for the first time ever.

"When I was a child, my parents disappeared in a plane crash over the Atlantic Ocean. My uncle – my father's brother – became my legal guardian. I spent fourteen years of my life terrified in my own home. He would hit me, push me, abuse me in almost every way possible."

She paused and took a deep breath.

"He did not sexually abuse me. In that regard, I suppose I am lucky."

Cat watched each Ranger's reaction to her story. Oliver squeezed his knuckles so tight she could see his skin turning white. Benjamin bit the inside of his cheeks in obvious rage. Wyatt's face had turned a deep shade of red.

"That mother—"

"Gray," Noah scolded, "there are children around."

"Just give me some C-4 and tell me where he lives," Wyatt muttered.

Once everyone had fallen quiet again, Cat continued her story.

"For years, my grandmother and I wrote each other. She always expressed her best wishes for my future – she'd ask me about my hobbies, my friends, my life. Eventually, I got tired of lying to her.

"The night before I called the local police to report my uncle, I had snuck out to a party with my friend Alannah. I had gotten so used to sneaking around the house, trying not to wake my uncle up, I thought I'd be okay getting back in.

But that night, I tripped and fell at the bottom of the stairs."

Cat could sense Noah's blatant anger steaming from his body, but she continued.

"I had woken him up. The last thing I remember before waking up in my own bed the next morning was him rushing at me and shouting. When I went to have a shower, I noticed a giant bruise on the back of my shoulder, and my head hurt."

A sudden grip on her hand pulled Cat's focus from her story. Her eyes darted to her hand – or rather, Noah's hand – as he caressed her from across the table. Cat could read what he was thinking from the look in his eyes.

You didn't tell me this.

Her heart beating to the pace of the music in the background, Cat refocused her attention back on the group.

"That morning, after I woke up, I was more terrified than I had ever been before. By seven that evening though, I was also happy. I was happy to watch the police officers escort him down our driveway and throw him into the back of the police car. I felt as though I could finally breathe again."

Cat choked on her final words, happiness and relief flooding her emotions. Noah's grip tightened for a split second, then eased.

"Address. Now. We'll show him the consequences for hurting such a beautiful young lady," Benji demanded. Oliver and Wyatt grunted in agreement, arms folded across their chests.

"There's no need," Noah interjected. "I showed up at Cat's house the following morning. Her grandmother had sent me to bring her back to America. Not long after we arrived in Athens, I received a call from the local police in Dunlavin – Cat's hometown. Her uncle had been murdered."

"Serves him right."

"Anyway," Noah continued, ignoring Wyatt's remark, "I brought Cat down to the precinct to ask her some questions about her uncle. When we returned to Margaret's house, she was dead. We later found out that she'd been killed the same way as Neil Gallagher – Cat's uncle. Since then, he's gone and killed a fellow cop."

A low, rumbling growl sounded from Wyatt's throat.

"Our clues have led us here, to Senator Mills. We found a note left behind by Margaret, which led us to his address."

He glanced at each of his men.

"There's more."

All three men leaned into the table, intrigued.

"It appears that the Senator's wife was killed recently. We think it has something to do with our killer."

"What do you need from us?" Oliver asked.

"The killer's next target is Cat. I need you three on protection detail and arms. I have to follow this investigation inside the boundaries of the law. Oliver, Benjamin, you'll be our backup, on us at all times. Wyatt, I'm going to need you and your resources. The FBI is bound to have a lot more techs and jurisdictions available to them than the APD do. As it is, this guy has already crossed state lines, not to mention international borders. You'll run lead on that end of things."

"Sounds good to me." Wyatt grinned. "Let's catch this son of a bitch."

***

After all of the plates had been cleared, Noah paid the bill, and everyone headed out to the SUV.

"Tell me about her, Gray."

Wyatt clapped his hands, pride in his voice.

"5.3 litre engine with 355 horsepower at 5,600 rotations per minute. Bulletproof windows and armour-plating. Nothing can withstand this beauty," he boasted.

"She'll do just fine," Noah said.

As his team climbed into the SUV, Noah felt a tug on his arm.

"Noah," Cat whispered, pulling him closer. "Why do they keep calling you Cap?"

"Because, sweetheart, I was discharged before I could make it to Major. I was their Captain."

Nodding, Cat smiled up at him and hauled herself into the car, Noah sliding in next to her.

"Next up, the Mills residence."

CHAPTER FOURTEEN

The dust on the grand piano scattered from the keys as Cat dusted her fingers gently over them one by one. It was obvious it hadn't been played in such a long time, which caused sadness to rise in Cat's heart. Her mother had taught her how to play piano when she'd been just a toddler. It was something she loved doing – creating beautiful music on such a magical instrument with her mother by her side. When her mother had died, however, Cat could never bring herself to play again.

"Do you play?" a childlike voice asked from behind her. "Mama used to teach us, but she's gone now."

Cat turned to find a little girl with plaited blonde hair – no older than six years old – staring up at her with deep brown eyes, waiting for an answer. The grief in those chocolate eyes spoke many words, reminding Cat of herself at that age – of the sadness that had once glossed her own eyes.

"I used to, when I was little, but I haven't played in a long time," she answered the girl, her voice soft.

Hope glistened in the little girl's eyes. She saw the opportunity to hear the piano played one final time, in memory of her departed mother, and Cat saw herself in the child.

"Will you play for me, please? It's been so long since it's been played. I really miss it."

Fear struck Cat then. It had been so long. What if she couldn't bring herself to create the music her mother had once praised. Or worse, what if she couldn't remember how to play?

Noah and Wyatt stood a few feet away, talking to the Mills' butler while they waited for the Senator to finish in a meeting. She watched the men for a few moments until, almost as if he could sense her gaze – her fear – Noah turned his head and shot her his usual foolish, comforting smile.

Somehow, the fear disappeared as quickly as it had come, fleeing Cat's subconscious and into the unknown. Her gaze fell back to the little girl. Though her heart raced in her chest, she felt empty – void – of worry, fear, and sadness. She hunched down so that she could meet the girl's eyes.

"I'll play on one condition," she said. The girl tilted her head to one side, curious as to what Cat could possibly want. "I'll play, if you play with me."

The girl opened her mouth as if to reject Cat's proposition, but quickly closed it and nodded her head compliantly. They seated themselves on the bench, backs straight, fingers resting on the keys.

"Which song would you like to play?" Cat

asked the girl.

She took a moment to think, and then said, "Do you know Für Elise? That was one of Mama's favourites."

"Okay. You ready?"

The girl nodded her head enthusiastically, hands at the ready. Cat gasped in a breath of air and slowly released it, closing her eyes and picturing the sheet music she used to use as a child. Her fingers began to press gently down on the keys, creating a soft melody – one she knew all too well. This piece had been her mother's favourite, too.

By the time she was four years old, she had nearly perfected Beethoven's composition. She opened her eyes when the little girl joined in. Her laughter was sweet as honey, and some amount of joy was brought back to her coloured cheeks.

The chatter behind them quieted down as they quickened their pace ever so slightly, paying little attention to the world outside the music. Cat knew all eyes were on her and the girl, but for the first time, she didn't mind it. In fact, she kind of enjoyed it. She was bringing joy to the little girl's day after she had lost her mother. Cat knew what that was like. She wanted to help the girl in any way possible.

The music enclosed her, swirling in a melodic breeze that only she could feel. She breathed it in, the sweet air of music. The little girl's bubbly laughter intertwined with the music, filling the room with a long-lost sense of happiness. Cat assumed that it had been a while since there was true joy present in this household.

Three minutes later, they drew to an end, finishing the composition on a happy note. As soon as the music ended, the little girl turned in her seat and threw her arms around Cat.

"Thank you so much, Miss!" she cried, drowning out the echoes of applause from the nearby men.

"No problem, little one."

Cat hugged the girl. She wished she could stay and help her. Show her that life goes on, that she would find happiness one day, even if that hadn't been Cat's experience until recently.

The girl hopped off the bench and over the butler and began tugging at his waistcoat. "Mr. Hanley, did you see what I just did? I played the piano!"

Cat giggled under her breath.

What a beautiful little soul.

"She hasn't been that happy since before her mother passed," a voice chuckled from the top of the stairs.

All heads in the room turned to the man now making his way down the stairs towards them. His lavish suit matched the muted colours of the foyer, and his age corresponded with much of the décor Cat had spotted around the vast room – old paintings, statues, knick-knacks. Cat had never seen such a grand home in all her life, even though her own house was big compared to most. Wrinkles spread thinly above his brows and grey streaks coloured his otherwise dark hair.

"Thank you, Miss…"

"Gallagher. Catarina Gallagher."

Reluctantly, Cat held out her hand to shake the man's. Though she wasn't over her fear, she had come to realise that she would never overcome it unless she worked on it – something she had learned after meeting Detective Noah Thompson and his friends.

As the man gripped her hand, introducing himself as Senator Hudson Mills, a kind of recognition crossed his aging face.

"Gallagher," he repeated, and he turned to greet Noah and Wyatt, leaving Cat with a growing curiosity.

"Senator Mills, I'm Detective Noah Thompson with the Athens PD in Ohio. And this is Special Agent Wyatt Gray with the FBI. We'd like to ask you a few questions about your wife if you don't mind."

***

Noah and Wyatt followed the Senator out of the foyer, through an archway and into a low-lit room. Books lined either side of the back wall, with a stone fireplace separating each side. Two musty armchairs sat at an angle on either side of the coffee table, facing away from the window and towards a long sofa directly opposite them. Noah examined the room with intense care. There were no hidden cameras, only one entryway into the room, and two average-sized windows facing out into the woods.

"Please, have a seat," the Senator said,

offering either armchair to the two investigators.

Noah swivelled in search of Cat, only to find her bee-lining straight for the oversized bookshelves. He could still feel the butterflies in his stomach from the melodic sound of the piano. He'd had no idea she had such a beautiful talent for music, though it didn't surprise him. The music rang in his ears as he watched her pluck books from the shelves, two at a time, reading each one eagerly, until she had an entire pile in her arms. A smile spread across his face, from ear to ear. Her beauty truly was endless.

The cushion under him curved to suit his physique, and he fell back into the chair.

"May I?" Cat asked the Senator, pointing at the hundreds of books covering the walls, as if asking now, after she had already pulled near twenty books from the shelves, was necessary.

"Of course, be my guest." The Senator smiled, obviously proud of someone else's interest in his collection, as he stacked firewood into the dwindling fire. He moved to the sofa across from Noah and Wyatt, keeping his smiling eyes on Cat as her love of books and literature became even more obvious.

"Meredith was like that too, you know. She absolutely adored reading," he said solemnly, his smile faltering. "I'm sorry, what was it you wanted to talk to me about again?" He shook his head and focused his attention on the two men sitting in front of him, notepads in their hands.

"Senator, you may find this hard to talk about, but we ask that you please give us as much detail as you can when answering our questions concerning your wife's death," Wyatt answered. "Anything – even the smallest piece of information – could be crucial to our investigation."

The Senator nodded his head, pressing his two palms together on his lap. Noah noticed the glistening fluid secreting from his skin. The Senator was nervous about something.

"Senator Mills, is it true that your wife, Meredith Mills, was found dead in your holiday home just outside the city six weeks ago?" Noah asked, maintaining his attention on the Senator's fidgeting hands.

The Senator's stare fell to the floor. He sighed in dismay.

"Yes, it is true. We managed to keep her death out of the media. It's a campaign year, you see, and she wouldn't have wanted to take away the publicity from the election campaign. But there was an official investigation opened by the local PD. Detective Cal Davison is the lead on the case," he answered.

Disgust laced Noah's next question.

"But do you not think that media coverage would have helped catch the killer, Senator? Surely that would be more important than getting re-elected?"

A short gasp sounded from the other side of the room, drawing Noah's attention for a moment. He had watched so many people in his life die, there was no way that he'd let the protection of his image give a murderer the chance to run free and kill more people. Unforgiving thoughts surged through his mind. There was the possibility that, if the Senator had run his wife's murder in the media, Margaret O'Donnell, Neil Gallagher, and a fellow officer would never have died. They could have caught the madman before he managed to kill again. Cat could have been happy, and safe.

Anger raged in the Senator's eyes, directed solely at Noah.

Wyatt spoke up.

"What my partner means to say is that we're sorry for the loss of your wife, Senator, and we would love to have as many people working on the case as possible. Your wife deserves justice for her untimely death."

The creases lining the Senator's face eased as he relaxed and turned to Wyatt.

"Thank you."

"Senator, why was your wife alone in the holiday home at the time of her death?" Wyatt asked.

The Senator's brows furrowed as he tried to think back to six weeks ago. After a few moments, his expression lit up.

"I remember her saying something about having to run an errand for one of the charities she runs and that she left something in the holiday home that she had to collect," he said at last.

"Do you remember which charity it was for, Senator?" Noah asked, drawing Senator Mills' glare back to him.

"No, Detective, I'm afraid I don't."

Noah looked to Wyatt, who gave him a forgiving smile. Noah knew it was his fault the Senator had closed off on them.

"Senator," Wyatt said, "would it be possible to get a list of all the charities your wife was a part of? Maybe it could help us find out why exactly she was there that day – maybe one of the charity staff knows something."

"I don't see why not, I suppose." Senator Mills shrugged, lifting himself from his seat and crossing over to the table next to the door. He pulled some paper and pen from one of the drawers and began to scribble on the page.

"Sorry about that," Noah whispered to Wyatt, though his eyes remained fixed on Cat, who was now hidden behind three tall piles of books, "It wasn't my intention to offend him. I just got..."

"Carried away in your own emotions?" Wyatt finished for him, one eyebrow raised.

Noah gulped, his gaze still fixed on the girl in the corner, smiling to herself.

"Yeah," he muttered.

Carpeted footsteps closed in around them until the Senator was sitting back on the sofa, holding out a folded parchment of paper between his grasping fingers.

"This is all of them," he said.

Noah took the list from him and began to read.

"Were there any charities that your wife was more involved in or were there any upcoming events around the time of her passing?" he asked.

"Actually, come to think of it, there were. The Women's Helpline and Mothers Inc foundations were founded by Meredith. If anything was as important to her as her work and her family, it was those two."

"Thank you, Senator, for your time," Noah said to the man, and he motioned to Cat, indicating it was time to go. To Noah's surprise, however, when Cat reached the archway, she spun on her heel and addressed Senator Mills again.

"Excuse me, Senator, but I couldn't help notice that you seemed to recognise my surname when I introduced myself. I was just wondering – did you know my parents by any chance? Emmett and Sarah Gallagher?"

Another flicker of recognition registered across the Senator's face.

"I haven't heard those names in years," he mumbled.

Noah's breath hitched at the unexpected answer. So, her parents had been on their way to Nashville, and whatever they were doing, the Senator may have been involved.

"You have to understand me, Miss Gallagher," Senator Mills continued, "I never personally met your parents. We had only ever spoken over the telephone."

"How did you know them?" Cat pressed.

Noah could hear her racing breath as she waited anxiously for an answer. He didn't dare move closer to her, as all attention was on the Senator as he answered her question.

"They called my wife – my, it must have been fifteen years ago – and started asking questions about some young boy. I had no idea what they were talking about at the time. It was only later that I discovered the truth."

Noah's eyes fell to the Senator's hands; he noticed that he was massaging his fingers anxiously. Beads of sweat slithered down his forehead, only to be caught by his bushy eyebrows before they could fall any further.

"When Mer was seventeen, she got pregnant by some man from Ireland while on vacation. He left for home before she found out and could tell him. So, she had the baby and gave it up for adoption.

"About nine years after the baby was born, she met me, and we were engaged to be married. A few days after we returned from our honeymoon, we received a phone call from your parents asking about the child. It appeared as though they wanted to adopt him and bring him home to Ireland.

"I wouldn't be able to tell you if Emmett Gallagher was the father of the child, though. All I know is that they were flying here to meet us and the foster parent the child was living with at the time, but they never arrived."

Cat looked to the floor, the words catching in her throat as she spoke.

"Their plane went down over the ocean on their way here. Their bodies were never found," she whispered.

"I am so sorry to hear that," the Senator

consoled her.

Her gaze jerked up from the floor, startling the Senator.

"Do you know what happened to the child?" she asked.

Senator Mills shook his head.

"I'm afraid not, I'm sorry."

After thanking the Senator for his time, Cat bid her farewells and made her way to the front door. As she passed by him, Noah held out a comforting arm, but she walked right past him without a word. Noah's heart felt heavy then, as he watched Cat hurry down the steps past Oliver and Benjamin, who looked bewildered by her speed, and pull herself into the dark SUV, slamming the door behind her. He hated witnessing such a beautiful, exuberant girl look so lost – so upset.

Holding back her tears only made Cat's sobs louder. Her parents had been coming here – to this very house. They had died trying to bring their son home and, in doing so, left both children without a family. Her heart bled for that little boy. He could have had a family. And she could have had an older brother – someone else to love.

Breathing became a struggle as Cat gasped for air between sobs. She watched Noah and the team walk towards her and the SUV through her mask of tears and closed her eyes.

Her lungs filled with air until there was no room left. She held her breath for three, two, one, and breathed out. One more time, she breathed in, and as she was releasing the air from inside her, the doors of the SUV opened, and the four men climbed into the vehicle.

"Are you alright?" Noah asked, gently wrapping his arm around her, then settling his hand on her arm. All eyes were on her. Concern, shock, sympathy, and love.

Love.

Was she falling in love with Noah?

Cat covered Noah's hand in hers and leaned into his shoulder, resting her head in the nook between his shoulder and neck. Her breath caught when she answered.

"I'm fine. I just... I never thought I'd ever find out the truth, y'know?"

Noah stroked her hair soothingly with his free hand.

"I know, sweetheart. And hey, if you want, we can try to find out who the kid was. Maybe you can meet your brother."

"That would be nice," Cat muttered. Her eyelids felt heavy under the weight of her relentless tears.

"Let's get you back to the motel, little lady. You can rest while the rest of the team try to figure out how to proceed with our new leads," Oliver said in a hushed tone.

"Okay."

With that, Cat's eyes drifted shut. Snuggling into Noah, she knew that she would be okay.

***

Anger dwelled deep inside Him. He watched the

girl hurry down the path and make her way into the SUV. Four men – all armed – shook the Senator's hand and made their way to her. Things were going to be a lot harder now.

They knew.

They knew about Meredith.

Soon, they would know about Him.

He pulled away from the side of the street and drove in the opposite direction to the SUV. He'd figure something out, but first, He had to disappear.

CHAPTER FIFTEEN

Diluted beams of light crept through the gaps in the curtains. The sun was rising in the east, and Noah and his team huddled together over the small table next to the window, talking in whispers, careful not to wake up a sleeping Cat.

Noah's weary eyes fell on the sleeping beauty. It had been days since she had gotten a good night's rest, and though she had uncovered some shocking secrets surrounding her family the day before, her exhaustion had finally overcome her, and she had not awoken once through the long night.

Noah forced himself to pull his attention from Cat and focus on his teammates.

"So, what have we got?" he asked Oliver and Benjamin, who stood across from him, notepads gripped tightly in their hands.

The two men looked to one another, silently deciding who would report back first. Benjamin gave a slight nod to his teammate who, in turn, set his notepad on the table for the entire team to see.

"I spoke to Diane Smith – the new chairperson for The Women's Helpline – and she said they didn't have any upcoming events until the end of summer. In all honesty, she wasn't much help at all."

Oliver massaged the back of his neck.

"It seems Mrs. Mills had become distant from the charity and the ladies involved. She hadn't been showing up to the weekly meetings. They hadn't heard from her in the weeks leading up to her death."

Noah scanned the lines of writing on the notepad with rapid speed.

"Do they know why she started to distance herself?" he asked.

Oliver shook his head.

"No. All they know is that it started two months ago."

"Well, that corresponds with what the woman from Mothers Inc told me," Benjamin whispered.

All eyes turned to him.

"Apparently, Mrs. Mills had been planning events nonstop for the foundation in the weeks leading up to her murder. Whether it was meetings, fundraisers, or even just a family picnic. They all thought she was overcompensating for something."

"Did you ask why?" Noah asked as he scribbled in his own notepad.

"This is where things get interesting," Benjamin answered. "She told them that her son had recently come back into the picture. She wanted to do everything with him that she had missed out on during his childhood."

"Her son? Did she mention a name?" Noah

glanced at Cat, who stirred at the sound of his voice.

If Mrs. Mills' son were in the picture, that would make him a suspect. Cat would be heartbroken to learn of her brother's involvement in a murder. All they needed was a name, and they'd finally have a solid lead.

"She said his name was Jack, or something like that. Mrs. Mills brought him to one of the meetings. They have a photo of her with her son. One of her friends from the foundation is meeting us at the Sky Blue Café at noon."

Wyatt's phone buzzed on the round table. All four men jumped for it in a bid to stop the violent noise from waking Cat from her slumber. Noah, being the first to reach it, grabbed the phone from the table and tossed it over to Wyatt, who mouthed a 'thank you' to him as he exited through the door.

***

Cat turned on her side and flicked her eyes open as the door clicked shut behind Wyatt. Noah and the others were gathered around the miniature table, whispering amongst themselves. She pressed the power button on her phone to check the time, but her attention quickly shifted to the sweet scent breezing her way, letting the screen go black again before she had the chance to look at the screen.

"What's that smell?" she asked, hands on her stomach.

All three men's heads turned to her. Noah lifted a brown bag from the table and handed it to her, sitting on the mattress beside her as she examined the bag's contents.

A clouded whiff of freshly baked waffles swirled beneath her nostrils. She inhaled, savouring the smell of honey and syrup.

Oliver grabbed a bottle of water from the mini-fridge and passed it to her with care, while Benjamin remained unmoving by the table, suddenly alert to the world on the other side of the window.

"What's going on?" she asked, pushing the first bite of breakfast into her mouth. It seemed as though Noah and his team were on high alert this morning. Even more so than usual.

"We have a lead," Noah answered. "Eat your breakfast, sweetheart. We're meeting a friend of Mrs. Mills' later today to get some answers."

Something in his voice led Cat to believe that he wasn't telling her everything. His face remained passive – almost as if he were deliberately trying to hide his emotions from her.

What was he hiding?

Cat's heart leapt in her chest. The thought of having a lead after so long...

The door opened, interrupting Cat's thoughts, and Wyatt entered the room, shoving his phone into his pocket. Noah looked at him expectantly as he closed the door behind him.

"That was Detective Davison with the MNPD. He's expecting us at the station in thirty minutes. He believes he might have information that will help our case."

Cat gulped down the last of her waffles and drank half of the water from the bottle Oliver had given her. Two leads in one day? Maybe things were finally starting to look up.

"Cat? Are you listening?"

A hand rested on the small of her back, pulling her from her daydream.

"Hmm? Yeah, sorry," she responded.

"I was just asking you how long you need to get ready to head out," Noah said, brows creased.

"Oh, sorry, I was in a world of my own," she laughed. "Give me ten minutes."

And she disappeared into the bathroom.

***

Noah followed Detective Davison into a poorly lit office, past the crowded desks of the officers of the Metropolitan Nashville Police Department. The room was small – so small that the only furniture in it was a desk and three small chairs. No filing cabinets. A window faced out into the lively city.

Stacks of opened files smothered the detective's desk. The smell of paper in the stuffy air churned Noah's stomach.

"You said you have some information that could help us, Detective?" Wyatt asked, cutting off Detective Davison's constant rambling apologies regarding the state of the room.

"Ah, yes," the detective said, lifting stacks of files from two of the chairs in the room. "Please, have a seat. And sorry again for the mess, we have a string of murders happening across the city."

Wyatt and Noah took him up on the offer, though they only sat on the edge of the cushioned seats.

"You're the lead investigator on the Mills murder?" Noah asked as he watched the detective study one of the many files on his desk.

"I am. Dreadful thing to happen to such a lovely woman. No one deserves to have their throat slit like that." Detective Davison shook his head in dismay. "So far, we only have one lead, but no name I'm afraid."

A sigh sounded behind Noah. He didn't have to turn around to know who had made the saddened sound.

"What's your lead?" Wyatt asked sternly, almost as if he were losing patience with the man.

"Word was that Meredith's long-lost son had come back into the picture after being given up for adoption twenty-seven years prior. We know that he introduced himself as Jack Harrelson, according to the diary we found belonging to Meredith Mills in the holiday home, but we couldn't find anyone registered with that name here in Tennessee or Arizona, where he claimed to have grown up. No birth cert, driver's licence, nothing. It's as if the man didn't exist."

Noah closed his eyes. This was exactly what they needed. A suspect who didn't exist.

"Is there anything else that can help us?" he asked.

"It was a closed adoption, but we're currently

working to get it unsealed. We should have it later today."

"Thank you, Detective. Let us know if you find any new information. We'll do the same."

Noah stood from the chair and walked from the office, through the precinct and out into the street without another word. The sound of honking cars drilled its way through his eardrums and lodged into his brain, sending a searing pain across his forehead. His eyelids felt heavy, and he was acutely aware of the dark circles beneath his eyes, but he wouldn't be able to have a good night's sleep until this guy was behind bars and Cat was safe.

"Noah! Wait! I can't run that fast!" Cat called out behind him.

By the time she had finally caught up to him, she was doubled over, hands on her knees, panting.

"You know I'm not great at chasing after people, right?" she laughed, trying to catch her breath.

"Sorry," Noah muttered. He didn't know what else to say.

"Look," Cat began, "I know more than anyone how badly you want to catch this son of a bitch. I do too. But you know what? I'm sick and tired of always feeling down and sorry for myself that we haven't caught this guy yet."

Cat's determined tone caught Noah by surprise. He turned and met her unwavering gaze and opened his mouth to speak. She held one finger up in the air, indicating that she wasn't finished talking yet.

"But we have something to go on now. We have *some* sort of lead, Noah, and that's more than we've had before. Does it sadden me to hear that my brother could be out there killing people? Of course it does. But there's still a person out there killing people – a person who needs to be caught. He can't hide forever. You're a good detective and I can tell how professional you and the others are at your jobs. We'll catch him. Besides, we still have to go and meet one of Mrs. Mills' friends, right?"

Noah struggled to push the words past his open lips.

Who was this girl standing before him?

Only a few days ago he had met this quiet, shy girl who, in all honesty, had let her emotions get the best of her. Yet here she stood, now, more adamant and confident than he found himself to be in that moment. Pride surged through every ounce of him.

She was facing her fears.

After a few moments, Noah realised that he hadn't answered Cat's question.

Well, that explained the discerning look on her face.

"Y-yes, yes. Sorry about that." He checked his watch. "We're meeting her in an hour."

"Are you okay?"

Cat stepped forward, cupping Noah's hands in her own.

Her skin felt soft against Noah's calloused fingers as she pressed against his body, keeping her gentle gaze on Noah.

"I'm okay. I was just, uh, surprised by your resolve to catch this guy. You're really starting to come out of your shell. I'm proud of you."

Heat flushed her cheeks, coaxing a smile onto Noah's lips.

"One thing I learned is that I'll never be who I want to be if I let my past get in the way. I learned that from you."

"Oh?"

Noah wondered what she could mean. As far as he was aware, he hadn't done anything to set an example. Before he could question her further on the topic, Oliver, Wyatt and Benjamin walked through the doors of the precinct.

"Well, well, well. What have we got here?" Wyatt smirked, eyes dancing between Noah and Cat. "Would you lovers like some privacy before we meet our next witness for coffee, or can you wait until we're back at the motel?"

This time, Noah's own cheeks flushed red, but his embarrassment quickly disappeared at Cat's unexpected response.

"Aw come on darlin', you jealous?"

Wyatt's mouth dropped open in shock. If one thing was for certain, he'd not expected a cheeky remark from Catarina Gallagher. And neither had Noah.

Oliver and Benjamin, however, burst into a fit of laughter, smacking Wyatt on the back as they applauded Cat's witty comeback.

"She got you there, Gray!" Oliver shouted above the laughter.

Shock prevented Noah from laughing, let alone speaking. Instead, he just stared at the girl still cupping his hands, admiration filling his heart. Cat turned back to him and winked.

Noah couldn't help but flash his foolish smile.

***

Cat stared at the woman sitting across from her as she nursed her coffee. She looked to be in her mid to late forties. She had fine golden locks, blue eyes, and was extremely pretty. Though it wasn't anything to be overly shocked about. From all the books she'd read growing up, wealthy women always read as drop-dead gorgeous *and* glamorous.

The past few minutes had passed in silence. Nobody said a word as the woman continued to sip her coffee, looking at each member of Noah's team with both a question of trust and a thirst of desire in her eyes. Cat couldn't blame the woman. They were all pretty fit.

Finally, the woman's eyes landed on Noah, and Cat felt the urge to set her hand over his on the table and interlock their fingers as a warning for the woman to back off, but she managed to restrain herself.

After a few more moments, Oliver grew impatient.

"Mrs. Carrols, can you please answer Detective Thompson's question," he demanded.

She set the empty cup of coffee on the table, lipstick marks evident on the lid, and turned her attention to Oliver.

"No, Jack didn't act suspicious in any way, shape or form. In fact, he was a real gentleman. He was always helping the girls out," she answered.

"What do you mean by 'helping the girls out'?" Noah asked.

"We're a charity, Detective. We rely on volunteers to get the work done, and we don't find many strong men volunteering to help us. Jack – or whatever his name is – carried in the heavy boxes and always helped us set up for events."

She stared at her perfectly manicured nails. Cat could feel the anger boiling in her stomach. Her friend had been murdered just weeks ago and as far as they knew this 'Jack' had killed four other people, and she was acting as if she didn't have a care in the world.

"Can you remember what he looked like, at least? This man has killed five people – he killed the only family I had left!" Cat cried out, drawing attention from the neighbouring tables.

The woman's eyes darted from her nails and landed on Cat. Her brows furrowed in a look of disgust at Cat's sudden outburst.

"Excuse me Miss I don't know who you think you are but–"

"Answer the question, Ma'am," Wyatt interjected, losing all sense of his gentlemanly behaviour he was so well known for.

The woman scowled at Cat, which turned into the brightest of smiles as she shifted her attention to Wyatt. Cat felt the light pressure of a palm on her shoulder. When she turned her head, she noticed Benjamin had risen from his seat and come around behind her. He tilted his head towards the entrance to the coffee shop, inviting her outside for some fresh air. Taking the hint, Cat got up from her seat and left the shop with Benjamin following closely behind.

As she reached the entrance, she looked back to the table and saw the woman slide a card across the table to Noah. Fury rose deep inside her at the thought of the woman slipping him her phone number after she had left the table.

"It's okay, you know," Benjamin said as they leaned against the SUV.

Cat spun her gaze from the window to the man standing next to her and looked up to meet his light green eyes.

"What's okay?" she asked, confused.

"To be jealous."

"I-I'm not..."

She sighed. There was no point in hiding anything from this man. He seemed to pick up on everything happening around him.

"Is it that obvious?" she asked quietly.

Though Noah wasn't near, she didn't want to risk anyone overhearing.

"Afraid so, sweetpea," he said with a smile. "To everyone except Cap, of course. He wouldn't know if a girl liked him if it smacked him in the face. Not until she told him, anyway."

"I see," was all Cat managed to say before Noah, Wyatt and Oliver burst through the doors in front of them.

"Get in the SUV. We have to get back to Athens *now*," Noah ordered, yanking the door open and ushering Cat into her seat.

"Whoa there, Cap, what's going on?" Benjamin asked as he climbed into his own seat on Cat's left side.

All doors slammed shut and Oliver pulled out onto the road, sirens blaring. Cat watched as Wyatt and Noah pulled phones from their pockets, pressed their speed dials, and held the phones up to their ears. Her stomach churned from the speed of the SUV as it flew down the road back towards the motel. Her heart was beating furiously in the cavity of her chest.

"What's going on?" she asked nobody in particular. She turned to Benjamin, who shrugged.

Her head whipped around to the other man sitting next to her. Noah spoke in quick words with the person on the other end of the phone.

"Blake, it's Noah. We know who the killer is."

***

Thoughts raced through Noah's mind.

How did they not realise it sooner? There had been so many hints.

They knew the killer would revisit the crime scene – that he would attend the funeral. They had a profile, yet they never thought to use it on those close to them – on people they knew.

Sure, why would they? There were no signs –

no evidence.

Noah held the picture card in his hand and stared at the one face he recognised.

***

Cat listened to Noah's frantic updates to Athens' Chief of Police, waiting to hear a name. There was something gripped between his fingers.

The card.

Without hesitation, Cat grabbed it from his clutches.

No.

It wasn't a card with a phone number on it.

A familiar face smiled back at her, almost as if he were taunting her. His dark brown, almost black eyes and his sandy blond hair made the hairs stand on the back of her neck.

A chill slithered down her spine.

He had tried to touch her that day. On the ambulance.

He had stood by her at her grandmother's funeral.

After all this time...

Cat stared at the picture in her hand, hatred in her gut, as Jackson Moore grinned back at her.

CHAPTER SIXTEEN

The bustling sound of the crowded offices muffled Noah's voice as he marched across the precinct floor with Evelyn and Blake matching his stride. After a seven-hour drive, his limbs felt heavy – sore – as if they were about to collapse from under him, and his voice strained with every word from the constant phone calls throughout the journey home.

They had driven through the night, with Noah and his team taking turns behind the wheel. But Noah hadn't been able to rest. After all this time, the killer had been someone hiding under his nose, in plain sight, within reach.

An hour before they had arrived in Athens, Blake had a warrant to search the paramedic's house, but he was nowhere to be found. His wardrobe was stripped bare, his door left unlocked, as if he knew they were coming, and he didn't care. Jackson Moore was in the wind, and they had no way to find him... yet.

"The adoption file came through ten minutes ago, just before you pulled up. It's waiting in my office," Blake said, though Noah had to strain his ears to hear him. "I'm heading out with Detective

Joy to question Moore's partner. I suppose it all makes sense now why her laptop was used to send that email."

The Chief of Police, followed by Noah's partner, veered off towards the entrance, leaving Noah alone with his thoughts.

This man – a paramedic no less, who had sworn to save lives – had taken the lives of five people. He had taken the life of Noah's dear friend and threatened a woman he'd grown to care for deeply. There was no way he'd get away with killing another soul. Not if Noah had anything to do with it.

Noah grabbed the file from the desk and was astounded at the weight of the paper. His eyes widened. It would take some amount of time to study it thoroughly.

What had Jackson experienced as a child?

Tucking the file under his arm, Noah stalked through the precinct one final time and climbed back into the SUV, where Cat and his men awaited him.

"Well? What does it say?" Wyatt asked, meeting Noah's bewildered gaze in the rear-view mirror.

Noah pulled the file from under his arm and held it up for Wyatt and the others to see.

"I don't know yet. The thing is the size of a lengthy novel."

"Oh, for fu–"

"Aghem," said Cat, stopping Wyatt before he could finish his sentence. "Where to now?"

She looked expectantly at Noah.

"First, Wyatt's going to drop us off at the Hampton Inn. We'll set up everything we have on Jackson so that we'll be ready to plan our op by the time you return."

"What do you mean op? And where am I going?"

A smile stretched across Noah's face.

"I thought you'd like to go and pick up that furry friend of yours yourself." He grinned.

Cat's face lit up like a Christmas tree, which only enhanced Noah's smile.

"He's ready to come home! It's about time!" she squealed, then leaned forward, gripping one hand on each of the front seats. "C'mon, Wyatt, can't you drive any faster!?"

"For you darlin', anything. But if I get pulled over, I'm telling them you coerced me," he laughed.

"Fair enough," Cat giggled. She was too excited to care.

Warmth covered Noah like a blanket on a cold snowy day at the sound of the pure happiness in Cat's voice.

The SUV slowed in front of a tall, brightly lit building. Noah waited for Benjamin and Oliver to exit the vehicle, before leaning into Cat's ear.

"Be careful, okay?" he whispered.

"I will, I promise," she whispered back.

Cat's skin felt hot beneath Noah's lips as he brushed them against her cheek and slid out from the vehicle.

"Watch over my girl, Gray," he called behind him.

***

Wyatt's grin revealed everything that remained unsaid as Cat brushed her fingers against the lingering kiss on her cheek. The luscious touch of Noah's lips had taken her by surprise and hearing him call her *my girl* as he left her sitting there, stunned, had caused butterflies to flutter around her stomach.

"He's never done anything like that before, you know," Wyatt said matter-of-factly.

"Hmm?"

Cat couldn't bring herself to speak. No one had ever kissed her before now – had ever claimed her as their own.

"Public affection," he explained. "He's not usually one for crushes, let alone relationships. Work has always been his priority – putting the bad guys away."

Wyatt's words drew Cat from her silent trance.

Noah wasn't one for romances?

The idea of never having a chance to love Noah caused Cat's heart to sink in her chest.

Aware of her silence, Wyatt perked up.

"But anyway, you're different. I can tell. Cap obviously likes you, and it's obvious how much you like him, too."

Cat didn't know how to respond. The fear of a life without her grandmother was beginning to subside. She knew her grandmother would only want the best for her. A life without Noah, however, she found hard to accept. This man was the only person in the world she felt close to, now that her family were gone. Cat chuckled under her breath.

Who knew that a man she had only met mere days ago would become such an important part of her life?

The car slowed and turned into a small car park off the side of the road. A small building surrounded by fields sat before them. Before Wyatt had gotten the chance to turn off the engine, Cat had unbuckled her seatbelt and was opening the door of the SUV.

"Whoa there, darlin', hold on a minute!" Wyatt said. "Let me check the surrounding area first. We don't know where this Jackson Moore is yet."

Cat released the door handle and sat back into her seat as Wyatt jumped down from the vehicle and scoured the area surrounding the vet clinic. Once he was sure that they were safe, Wyatt doubled back to the SUV and helped Cat onto the ground.

"Thank you." Cat smiled at her new friend. As tall, witty, and handsome as Supervisory Special Agent Wyatt Gray was, he was also a true professional gentleman.

Inside the vet clinic, dogs barked and cats meowed. Cat knew she wouldn't be able to hear Shep, though. He was never really one for barking. Excitement burst from Cat's chest as she approached the young man behind the front desk.

He smiled. "Good afternoon, how can I help

you today?"

His body straightened in his seat, and he leaned forward over the desk – an attempt to maximise the connection with another human being. It was clear that this young man was happy to have someone other than the animals to talk to.

"Hi!" Cat said. "I'm here to collect Shep. He's a two-year-old border collie."

Cat set her bag on the desk and scoured its contents. After a few moments, she pulled out Shep's documents and handed them over to the man.

"One moment please," he said, and disappeared through a door into the clinic.

Cat couldn't help but smile foolishly. The past few days without her best friend had been rough.

"Border collie, eh?" Wyatt said from where he stood by the front door. He occasionally peered through the window for any signs of a threat.

"Yeah!" Cat beamed. "My dad's dad – my granddad – used to own a sheep farm. I'd go down every weekend when my uncle would want rid of me and help out with the feeding and everything. He had a few sheepdogs for herding and quilling and the likes. Shep was the last gift I ever got from him before he passed a few years back."

Wyatt arched his brows in amazement.

"I know, I don't exactly come across as a farm girl, what with the money and all, but I would take a farm in the country over living in the city any day."

"Whoa boy, hold on!" the young man called

from behind the front desk, but before he could say another word, Cat could hear the pattering of paws on the wooden floor. She found herself laughing as the big furball she loved so dearly hopped over the desk and jumped into her arms.

"Hey boy," she chuckled, "I see you're still causing trouble." She looked to the man panting behind the desk. "Sorry about that. How much do I owe you?"

"Um, the bill's already taken care of, ma'am," he said, sitting back at his computer.

"Oh? By whom?" Cat asked. Surely Noah didn't pay the bills by himself. She could easily manage to pay for her own dog's health.

Fingers tapped at the keyboard.

"By a Jackson Moore, ma'am."

***

Noah dropped his go bag onto the large bed on the opposite side of the suite, pulled out his laptop and doubled back to the others in the living room. Constant shivers coursed through Cat's body where she sat next to Wyatt, who was petting the dog that lounged on his lap.

Noah rounded the sofa and sat next to the girl he'd grown to care for deeply. He opened his laptop with one hand while he wrapped the other around Cat, pulling her closer to him.

"Tell me again what the vet said, sweetheart. Word for word."

He pressed a gentle kiss on the top of her head, hoping it would ease her shaking.

"The day after Shep was brought in, a man who called himself Jackson Moore phoned the clinic and paid the bill by card." Her head whipped to the side, and she pressed her face into the crevice of Noah's shoulder. Noah could feel the threat of tears welling in her eyes. "Noah, if he hurt Shep…"

"He didn't, sweetheart. It's okay. We're going to catch him, I promise."

Fury raged deep within the pit of Noah's stomach and rose up to his chest. His blood boiled to a point that turned his face a deep shade of red. Jackson Moore would be lucky if he made it out of this alive; cop or no cop, Noah wanted to kill him for what he'd put Cat through.

"Hold on a minute," Oliver said. "If he paid by card, we could track his movements. Maybe we'll get lucky, and he used his card after he disappeared."

"I'm on it."

Benjamin pulled his own laptop out of a bag resting at his feet and was soon tapping away at the keys, silently listening to the others.

"What else do we know about him?" Wyatt asked, refusing to take his gaze from the dog.

"Why is it that the dog seems to like everyone but me?" Noah sulked.

Cat giggled and he realised that her head was still resting on his shoulder, which caused his heart to swoon. She looked so beautiful. He could really get used to that view.

"Because, Cap, you're just an old grump when it comes to animals. They never like you," Wyatt teased.

"Oh yeah?" Noah retorted. "Well what's so good about you then?"

A muffled scoff drew Noah's attention to the two men sitting across from them. Oliver and Benjamin averted their eyes from his glare, covering their mouths with their fists and faking coughs to hide their amusement.

"All you need is a gentle touch," Wyatt mused. "Don't worry, Cap, you'll learn the skill eventually. You just don't have years of experience living on a ranch in Wichita Falls surrounded by these beautiful creatures like I do."

"You had sheepdogs?" Cat asked, pulling away from Noah's embrace.

"Sure did, darlin'. Though we had cattle rather than sheep."

"That's awesome!" Cat remarked.

"Cap."

Benjamin's voice banished all amusement from the room. Noah dropped his pouting act and snapped back into cop mode.

"What is it, Benjamin?"

"Moore used his credit card less than two hours ago in Belmont County."

"What's he doing there?" Oliver asked, leaning in closer to get a better look at the laptop screen. Noah picked a file from the table – Jackson's file Blake had gotten written up while they were on their way back to Athens.

He scanned the file, reading it aloud to the others as he did.

"Jackson Moore. Twenty-seven years old. Hometown: Tucson, Arizona. Current residence: Athens, Ohio. Other than that, we only have his current residence and workplace. Most of the other pages are job applications, his certificate for the completion of his EMT training..."

Noah flicked through the lengthy file. School records, job and housing referees, house and car insurance. No note of his family, his childhood. And nothing out of the ordinary.

How could you be friends with someone but not know anything about them?

There would be one person, however, who knew the man they were looking for. Noah passed the file to Oliver – who proceeded to examine each page himself – then grabbed his phone and dialled his partner's number. He pressed the phone to his ear.

"Lyn, I need you to do me a favour. You still with Jackson's partner? Great. Bring her to us. There's no way she worked with him for an entire year and never learned anything about him. They were too close. You know where we're staying. Be careful."

"You really think Maria could know something? Cat asked quietly.

Noah nodded.

"You can't work with someone for so long and not know anything about their life, but we'll keep digging, too."

With that said, Noah's laptop *binged*.

Resting it on his lap, Noah opened his email to find an attachment to a folder forwarded to him straight from the MNPD. He looked up from his screen to find everyone staring at him, waiting patiently. If the circumstances weren't so dim, Noah would almost find it funny.

"It's from Detective Davison. Looks to be Jackson's adoption paperwork," he told them.

"Well, let's start reading," Wyatt declared.

***

A soft knock on the door pulled Cat's attention from the file in her hands. Noah and Wyatt stood up and drew their weapons. Without a sound, and pointing their guns at the floor, they approached the door to the suite. Wyatt, standing against the wall, weapon at the ready, nodded at Noah, who proceeded to yank the door open and aim his Sig at the visitors.

"Whoa there, Thompson, stand down," came a familiar voice from the hallway. Noah holstered his weapon and stood back, allowing the two women to enter the room. Cat watched them come into view.

Evelyn stood close to the female paramedic, who kept her eyes on the floor. Cat stood, refusing to look away from the obvious expression of guilt on her face. Hesitantly, she stepped towards Maria. It felt as if she were drifting across the floor on a soft cloud.

It didn't feel real.

Had this woman known what her partner was doing all this time? When he must have disappeared for hours at a time, had she noticed?

"Maria," Cat whispered.

The woman broke down into furious tears.

"I'm so sorry, Cat. I'm so *so* sorry."

She pounced forward and wrapped her quivering arms around Cat's body. Noah and Wyatt, who were watching from a few feet away, made a move to tear Maria from her, but Cat raised her hand and silently shook her head once. Though the men stood down, the tension in their muscles and anger in their eyes betrayed their otherwise passive expressions.

Sucking in a deep breath, Cat wrapped her arms around Maria with care.

"What happened, Maria?" she asked coolly.

A dramatic sniff, and Maria separated herself from Cat. Evelyn stepped closer, placing her body in the space between them.

"I-I loved him. I know I w-wasn't supposed to b-but I did," she cried horrendously.

"It's okay, Maria. Try to take a deep breath. Follow my lead." Cat breathed in. "One." And out.

"Okay, again," she said, air filling her lungs. "And out."

When they reached a count of four, Maria's cries had turned to sobs, and when she spoke, her words were easier to understand. Cat knew that she should be upset with this woman — furious even — but instead, all she saw was another victim of abuse. Sure, it didn't seem as though Maria had any bruises on her skin as far as she could see, but Cat could tell just how much this woman had suffered emotionally during her time with Jackson Moore. She felt sympathy for the woman.

"Would you like a bottle of water?" Cat asked her as she led her to the sofa.

Maria nodded her head eagerly.

"Yes, please."

"I'll get it," Evelyn said.

Cat and Maria lowered themselves onto the empty sofa. Cat's arms embraced Maria, holding her close, and she laid her head on top of her friend's.

"I know this is hard, Maria, but you're safe now. He's not going to be able to hurt you anymore," she whispered.

A short gasp as Maria pulled away from Cat, then, "How did you know?"

Cat's chest tightened as she thought of her answer, remembering all of those painful memories.

"It's easier to tell when you've been through it yourself. I'm sorry I didn't notice sooner."

"No," Maria sobbed. "Please. It should be me apologising to you. I knew something was wrong with Jackson. I saw that email he sent from my laptop. But, but..."

She trailed off, unable to finish her sentence. Cat knew what she was going to say.

But if I told anyone, he'd hurt me.

"It's okay. I understand," Cat soothed, hugging her tight. "You're safe now."

Oliver pushed himself to the edge of his seat and stretched his arm out over the table.

"Maria," he said quietly, "I'm Oliver Campbell. Are you hurt anywhere?"

Maria stared at the man sitting across from

her and looked right into his forgiving hazel eyes.

"Oliver's our medic," Noah told her.

A few moments of silence. Maria held her gaze on Oliver, who offered her a sympathetic smile.

"I'm not hurt," she said at last. "Not physically, at least."

Oliver's smile faded as he rested his large hand on her knee and said, "I'm here if you need me."

"Maria," Cat spoke up, drawing the paramedic's attention back to herself. "We're going to need you to tell us about Jackson. As much as you can. Can you do that for us?"

Maria nodded her head, but kept her eyes fixed on Oliver's hand, which was still patting her knee.

Cat glanced back at Noah, who gave her a curt nod and flipped open his notepad.

"He-he was adopted when he was two. He lived in Tucson, Arizona until he was seventeen. Something happened to his adoptive parents. He never told me what, exactly – only that his father was a doctor and he wanted to follow in his footsteps one day. He ran away before social services could place him in the foster system. He worked, saved up money, and trained to join the fire department as a paramedic."

"Has he seemed off lately? Did anything happen out of the ordinary?" Cat asked.

Maria jerked her head and turned her body to meet Cat's, her eyes frantic.

"What is it, Maria?" Noah pressed.

"About two months ago, Jackson received a letter in the mail. All I know is that it mentioned something about his birth mother. He never told me anything more than that."

"Do you know where the letter is now?"

"Y-yes, I think so."

Noah swung his notepad closed and pocketed it.

"Wyatt, go with Evelyn and Maria, see if you can find the letter or anything else that might help us find Jackson." He turned his attention to the men still sitting in the armchairs. "Benjamin, see if you can find anything online about a Moore family living in Tucson, Arizona around ten to twenty years ago. Oliver, we're going to go through the adoption file again. Leave no stone unturned."

"What about me?" Cat asked. "What can I do?"

"Get some rest, sweetheart. Things are only going to get more tense from here."

Noah caressed Cat's hair, then leaned over and planted a soft kiss on her forehead.

He watched her disappear into the bedroom before refocusing his attention on the task at hand.

"What exactly are we looking for, Cap?" Oliver said.

"Anything that can help Benjamin find Jackson's family," Noah responded, opening the file and beginning to read it over again.

Fifteen minutes passed before Noah found anything of interest.

"Dustin Moore..." he muttered.

"What's that?" Benjamin peered over his laptop screen at Noah, waiting expectantly for an answer.

"Dustin Moore. He was Jackson's adoptive father. Something about the name sounds familiar, like I should recognise it."

"I recognise it too," Oliver murmured.

Benjamin disappeared behind his laptop. For two minutes, the only sound in the room was the tapping of keys until, "I know why he sounds familiar."

He sat the laptop on the table and spun the screen around for his teammates to see. Noah's eyes widened and his jaw dropped as he read the title of the article.

"How didn't I see it before!"

"See what?" Oliver asked.

"The pattern. The M.O. It's the same. A slice across the throat with a scalpel, cutting the jugular." Noah could feel his heart drumming against his ribcage – he could hear the thumping in his ears. "Jackson's killing people the very same way his father did fifteen years ago. Eighteen victims over the span of eleven years."

"Holy shi–"

"Where's he detained, Benjamin?"

After a few more taps at the keyboard, Benjamin handed his laptop to Noah.

"Belmont Correctional Institution. They were only able to nail him on the murder of two sisters missing from St. Clairsville a few years back."

Noah sighed deeply.

"Well then, it looks like I'm going to St. Clairsville, Ohio."

CHAPTER SEVENTEEN

Noah felt as if a part of him was missing as he placed his Sig Sauer P320 into the security box the prison officer held in his hands. It was rare that he was without his weapon, whether he was on duty or off. As far as he was concerned, it had become an extra limb.

As far as we're aware, Dustin Moore hasn't had any communication with the outside world in months," the warden told him as they passed through the prison. "His son – I can't remember his name–"

"Jackson Moore."

"Yes, that's it. Well, the last time Jackson visited, his father gave him a letter – which we examined, mind you – but we didn't find anything suspicious or dangerous inside. It was just a letter regarding his biological parents."

"Oh, it was dangerous alright," Noah muttered under his breath.

"What was that, Detective?" the Warden asked.

He opened the single door at the end of the hallway, revealing an older man in an orange jumpsuit sitting at a table, his cuffed hands resting on top.

"Nothing," Noah answered as they entered the room.

The man, who had been slouched in his chair, straightened at the sight of Noah's badge on his hip. The corners of his lips curled upwards into a knowing, torturous smile.

"Who's this, Warden?" the convict asked coyly, keeping his intrigued gaze fixed on Noah.

"Detective Noah Thompson with the Athens Police Department," Noah answered before the warden had the chance to open his mouth. He needed to show this man that he was someone to be reckoned with.

"Athens, eh? I haven't been there in some time. I bet the young ones there are prettier than ever," he crooned. "Do you have one, Detective? A pretty little thing?"

Dustin Moore's eyes betrayed his otherwise innocent tone.

Noah clenched his fists at his sides and bit the inside of his cheek. He couldn't let this psycho get to him. Not when he needed answers – information that could help him find Jackson. He sucked in a deep breath and unclenched his fist. He stepped forward and slowly pulled the chair opposite the convict out from under the table. He never broke eye contact with Dustin.

Once he was settled, he dropped his notepad onto the table and clicked.

"So serious," Dustin Moore said with a smirk.
"Mr. Moore–"
"Please, call me Dustin," the man

interrupted.

Noah showed no acknowledgement that he had spoken and continued.

"Mr. Moore." The convict's smile faltered. "Where is your son? Where is Jackson Moore?"

Noah's voice remained passive. He could not let this man know that he was emotionally involved. For now, he'd have to play cop, rather than friend.

"I have not spoken to my son in months, Detective. Why do you want to know?" Dustin answered, sticking his chin up at Noah, suspicion laced in his voice.

"We know you gave Jackson a letter regarding his biological parents several months ago. Since then, your son has murdered his birth mother, among others. So, I'll ask you again, Mr. Moore: when was the last time you saw your son?"

Noah was becoming agitated. If he didn't find a way to quell the anger raging inside him soon, he'd give himself away. He pictured himself resting on the sofa, Cat sleeping in his arms as he held her close. The thought of embracing her – to be able to call her his – warmed his heart. He unclenched his fists and palmed the table, a stern look in his eye.

Dustin Moore's expression lit up.

"He killed someone you loved, didn't he?" It was more of a statement than a question. "I'll tell you about my son if you tell me – in detail – what he did."

Air caught in Noah's throat.

Thank God Cat wasn't here for this, he thought, though he wouldn't imagine she'd be happy that he'd left while she was sleeping, either.

"Fine," Noah said at last, leaning back in the chair. His stomach churned at the thought of describing Margaret's murder to this sick bastard, but it was the only option he had if he wanted Jackson Moore off the streets as soon as possible.

"Her name was Margaret O'Donnell..."

***

Cat awoke to the sound of knuckles tapping quietly on the bedroom door.

"Come in," she yawned, stretching her arms above her head.

Benjamin pushed the door open with his boot, a tray topped with food balanced in his arms.

"Breakfast is served," he announced.

"Aw Benji, you shouldn't have." Cat smiled, eagerly taking the tray from him. Pancakes, fruit, and orange juice. One of Cat's favourite breakfasts. It was sweet of Benjamin to bring her breakfast in bed.

Almost too sweet.

Suspicion laced Cat's next words.

"What's going on?" she asked him.

"Why can't a man just bring a pretty lady like yourself breakfast in bed?" he answered, his cheeks turning a bright shade of pink.

"I suppose. But if anyone would be bringing

me breakfast in bed, I would have guessed it to be Noah." Cat set the tray on the bed and slid out from under the sheets. "Where is Noah, anyway?" She peered through the open doorway, but in the time it took her to blink, Benjamin had moved in the way, blocking her view.

"About that..."

"Benji," Cat drawled his nickname.

"He's gone to visit Jackson's father in prison. He'll be home by tonight," the sniper spat out. "Sorry we didn't wake you. He wanted us to keep you safe, here, where we could protect you."

"Benjamin Myers—"

"Uh oh." Benjamin massaged the knots on the back of his neck.

"You're telling me that you let Noah go off to who knows where to do who knows what *on his own*, without backup, to protect me? Surely it doesn't take three of ye to protect me – at least one of you could have gone with him."

"Uh, yeah, I guess that would have made more sense..."

Cat folded her arms across her chest.

"Well, you are a clan of clowns now aren't ye," she noted, her Irish accent becoming more evident.

"Huh?" Benjamin tilted his head, confusion masking his face.

"Nothing." Cat rolled her eyes. "Listen, can I ask a favour?"

She approached the former Ranger. A bead of sweat raced down his forehead.

Did she make him nervous?

"On the off chance that something happens to me, I'd like to be able to defend myself. Can you teach me a few moves?"

The tension in Benjamin's shoulders eased and he became much more relaxed.

"Sure thing. What would you like to know?"

***

Noah's eyes slitted into a glare as Dustin Moore's gaze filled with sick pride. A smirk crossed the convict's chapped lips, which almost sent a shiver down Noah's spine. Dustin Moore was a sadistic excuse of a human being, that much Noah was sure of, but Noah had faced worse in his years as a Ranger.

Bile slithered its way up his throat. The vivid images of his old friend's murder were, once again, fresh in his mind. Retelling the story didn't help much in banishing the dirty smell of blood oozing from her fresh corpse.

"That's my boy," Dustin snickered.

Noah had had enough. This bastard had promised him answers and Noah planned on getting them, by any means necessary.

"Enough, Moore," he declared. "I told you my story, now you tell me what I want to know."

Dustin's snicker transformed into a wide grin.

"Alright, Detective, whatever you wish."

He leaned on the table, closing the gap between them.

"Twenty-six years ago, my good-for-nothing

wife decided she wanted a baby, but we couldn't conceive. So, we adopted a little boy – Jackson." Dustin yawned. "It didn't take long for her to decide that she didn't like parenthood, so, she tried to leave."

"Tried?" Noah interjected.

"Yes, Detective, tried. As in, she didn't succeed." He smiled. "Anyway, I was a surgeon at the time, so it wasn't difficult finding the best way to dispose of the body. Jackson, unfortunately, saw it all."

Noah scribbled in his notepad, holding on to every word the man said.

"She was my first. A few years later, I quit my job, sold the house, and travelled around the States with my son, teaching him the ins and outs of the perfect murder."

Dustin licked his lips.

"One smooth slice across the jugular and they'd bleed out in minutes," he moaned.

Noah forced back an involuntary gag.

"Eleven years we got away with it. That is, until those twin bitches from St. Clairsville. We would have gotten away with that too if it weren't for Blake Richardson."

Noah's head jerked up from his notes.

Blake? What did he have to do with the Clairsville Twins case?

"What is it, Detective? Recognise the name?" he teased.

Noah pushed the new piece of information from his mind. He'd have a chat with Blake when he returned to Athens.

"Just tell me about Jackson so we can get this over with."

He refocused his stare back to his pen and paper.

"He was seventeen when I got locked up. He avoided foster homes until he came of age. We kept in touch, and I kept teaching him everything he needed to know."

Dustin paused.

"I bet he's in the wind now. Oh no, you'll never find him. Not unless he wants you to."

Noah stood from his seat, closed his notebook, and pocketed it.

"One last thing," he said, maintaining eye contact. "Does the name *Gallagher* mean anything to you?"

Recognition breezed across the older man's face.

"They contacted me when Jackson was twelve years old. Wanted to know if I'd allow them to take him away to Ireland. Family, they said he was, and that he needed to be with people related by blood. Promised they'd look after him, but they weren't his parents. No, Meredith Johnson and Neil Gallagher were the names on the birth certificate."

So, Jackson Moore was Cat's cousin, not her brother.

Noah showed no reaction to Dustin's statement.

"What did you say to the Gallaghers?" he asked.

"I said no," Dustin answered disgustedly. "So

they wanted to fly to the States to meet me and Meredith, but I never heard from them again."

Noah scowled.

"Because they died trying to get to him – to take him in as their own."

Dustin spat on the floor.

"Good riddance."

Noah stepped forward as the urge to wrap his hands around Dustin Moore's neck overpowered him, but he quickly thought better of it. Instead, he turned on his heel and strode out the door.

***

Cat's fists slammed against the padded shield; first her right, then her left. Sweat flowed down her forehead. The room had become too hot.

"That's it, now kick," Benjamin enthused.

Cat turned on her left heel, transferring all her weight to that side, and sent her right foot into the air, making contact with Benjamin's leg.

Her hands clasped over her gaping mouth.

"Oh my – I'm so sorry Benjamin!" she said.

Benjamin, gripping his knee, attempted a smile and said through his gritted teeth, "Nice kick."

Colour drained from Cat's cheeks, lightening the red tint scattered across her cheeks from the heat.

"I think we'll leave it at that for today. Go shower," Benjamin hinted, letting go of his sore knee.

"Okay. Sorry again," Cat repeated.

By the time Cat had showered, dressed, and was sitting down to dinner, the sun had set behind the skyline. She sat at the table with Oliver, Benjamin and Wyatt, and though they conversed amongst themselves, Cat found herself unable to take her mind off Jackson Moore.

She stabbed the cooked chicken sitting helplessly on her plate with her chopsticks. Hand in her palm, she stared into oblivion. In the time she had been in America, her grandmother – the last remaining member of her family – had been killed, she had been in a car accident, she had found out she had a long-lost brother – who was the reason for her parents' sudden trip across the ocean, which had resulted in their deaths – and now she was in a whole new world she didn't know with no place to go.

"Excuse me," she whispered, pushing her plate further away from her and rising from the table.

"You okay?" Benjamin asked, standing up in his own seat across from her.

"I'm fine," Cat lied. "I'm just tired is all. I'm going to head to bed. Night."

Benjamin hesitated, providing Cat with enough time to escape to her room.

Closing the door behind her, Cat fell onto the firm bed and blinked back the tears welling in her eyes. Her old photo album rested where she had left it on the bedside table. All her memories long forgotten.

She grabbed the album and pushed herself into a sitting position, laying it open across her thighs as she instinctively settled her fingers on a sleeping Shep's coat. Cat stroked the first photo with her thumb; a picture of a new-born baby in the arms of her loving mother, her father holding her hand. Tears burst through Cat's tired eyes. She couldn't hold them back any longer.

She flipped through page after page, admiring each photo, remembering her happy childhood. After ten minutes, Cat found herself staring at the photo of her mother on her wedding day and hoped that one day she too would find happiness like her mother had found with her father. She believed that she might have already met the person she'd like to spend the rest of her days with, but she didn't know if he felt the same way.

Cat studied her mother's locket as her heavy eyelids fluttered closed. As the calming darkness began to surround her, she remembered one final thing: her mother's final piece of advice.

"No matter what happened, the answer will always be close to your heart."

***

The door clicked quietly behind Noah as he tiptoed into the suite. The sun had set hours ago, and Noah's body ached for a bed to lie on. After putting his bag on the sofa, he turned and started towards Cat's room, only making it several steps before reaching for his weapon.

A shadowed figure sat in the chair outside her door, watching Noah's every move.

"Relax." The figure switched on the lamp at his side, illuminating his face. "It's just me."

The tension in Noah's muscles relaxed. Distancing his hand from his weapon, he asked, "How is she?"

"Asleep," Oliver said. "Has been for a few hours now."

Noah stepped closer.

"I'm going to check on her, then I'll take over here."

Oliver opened his mouth to protest when Noah added, "That's an order, Lieutenant."

Oliver nodded grudgingly.

Silently, Noah opened the door to Cat's room, only to find her curled up on the bed next to the dog, asleep with the light still on. He couldn't help but smile.

His movements remained inaudible as he made his way across the room. An open photo album lay askew on the floor. Cat must have been looking through it when she fell asleep.

As gently as possible, Noah lifted Cat in his arms and pulled back the comforter. She didn't so much as stir. Noah placed her in the bed and tucked her in, placing a soft kiss on her forehead before exiting the room and settling himself into the empty armchair outside her door, watching for any signs of a threat.

CHAPTER EIGHTEEN

Something nuzzled against Cat's cheek, tingling her skin, and pulling her from her nightmares. She knew she had been tossing and turning through the night, but, looking now, she wondered how she ended up under the warmth of the comforter.

Weird.

Another nuzzle against her skin, followed by a quiet whine, drew Cat's attention to her furry companion, who was desperate for some love.

"Good morning, Sheppy. How are you today?" Cat laughed.

Embracing his head in her hands, she placed a quick peck on his wet nose and climbed half-heartedly from the bed. As she stretched, Cat sucked in a deep breath, allowing the sweet aroma of coffee to fill her nostrils.

"Let's eat," she said, and she started after Shep, who had pattered from the room. After taking a single step towards the door, however, pain darted from her toes and travelled up through her nervous system.

"Ouch!" Cat yelped.

Hopping on one foot, Cat scoured the floor in

search of a deadly weapon, only to find her old photo album lying next to the bed. Slowly, she released her foot from her grasp, straightened her stance, and let her mouth fall open.

"Oh shit."

With all the speed she could muster, she dashed from her room and into the suite, her eyes darting from room to room.

No sign of Noah.

The bustling of pots and pans from the kitchen drew her attention.

"Wyatt!"

"Oh fu–"

A loud pang erupted through the suite as a large pan hit the floor.

Cat sighed, already gasping for air.

"Where's Noah?"

Shocked, Wyatt remained silent for a moment. Words had failed him. Instead, he pointed to a closed door on the opposite side of the kitchen. Cat nodded her thanks, ignoring the man's gobsmacked expression, and rushed to the door.

Without knocking, she burst through the door and into the bathroom.

"Noah! Noah! I figured it–"

Toned olive skin caught Cat's innocent gaze. Noah stared at her, wide-eyed, unable to force a single word past his lush lips. She scanned his body, which remained bare before her. Staring at his broad shoulders – which glistened beneath leftover water droplets from the shower – Cat's gaze dropped to the curved dents of his collar bones, the strong biceps, and onto his well-defined abs that would make any girl drool. Her eyes settled on Noah's abdomen for what felt like hours, and she found herself unable to tear them away – to look anywhere but at this man's strapping body. Though temptation begged her to, Cat did not dare look any lower.

"Oh! Sorry!" she exclaimed quickly, turning to face the wall.

Colour flushed her cheeks. She was grateful that Noah couldn't see her reflection in the tiled wall before her.

"It's okay," Noah said, a hint of humour in his voice. "You can turn around now."

Covering her cheeks with her hands to hide her rosy colouring, Cat turned to face Noah once again, only this time to find him wrapped in a towel.

"What was it you wanted to tell me so badly it couldn't wait?" he chuckled.

Cat watched his chest expand with each breath he took.

"Oh, um..."

She scrunched her nose as she wracked her thoughts that remained stashed behind the images of Noah's naked body.

"Oh yeah! I think I've figured out what Jackson's after!" She clutched her locket in her hands like she had done so many times before. "And it has something to do with this!"

***

Gathered around the table, Noah, Cat, Benjamin, Wyatt and Oliver all stared at the open locket lying before them. Inside rested an old photo of Emmett and Sarah Gallagher holding a new-born admiringly in their arms.

"Is there anything else – something behind the picture, maybe?" Benjamin asked, looking over to Cat for an answer.

Cat shook her head.

"No. I've looked at that picture more than a thousand times over the years. There's nothing else," she explained, feeling her heart sinking. All the excitement had drained from her system. Surely, this had to be what Jackson was after, right? It was the only thing he hadn't been able to get his hands on yet. But what was so special about it to him?

Noah hovered his hand over the locket.

"May I?" he asked.

"Of course," Cat said.

With a gentle touch, Noah lifted the locket in the palm of his hand and examined it closely – every corner, the colour of the ink, everything he could think of.

"Something looks off here," he whispered, more to himself than to anyone else. As carefully as he could manage, he peeled the old photo from its place in the locket and set it down on the table. "Here, look."

One by one, each member of Noah's team leaned closer to the photo.

"The paper, it's not the typical kind used for photographs?" Wyatt questioned as he stroked the parchment with his index finger. "Is there anything on the back?"

"Nothing," Cat answered. "Not unless there's some sort of secret message hidden somewhere."

She sighed.

"That's it!" Noah exclaimed.

He rushed from the room, only to reappear several moments later, goggles in his hand.

"Benjamin, pull those curtains. Oliver, close every door that lets light into the room."

Once all light had been extinguished from the room, Noah pulled his UV goggles over his eyes, peered down at the paper, and gasped.

"What? Noah, what is it?" Cat asked frantically.

"It looks like code, but I don't know."

Noah pulled the goggles over his head and handed them to Cat.

"Somebody wrote a message on the back of the photo in invisible ink. Whatever it is, they didn't want it found," he explained to the others.

A short gasp sounded from beside him.

"They're bank account details. The first line, that's an IBAN. It's the system we use in Ireland – hence the 'IE'. The second row is the account number," Cat said, her breath shaky. "Is this what Jackson's after? I never even knew it existed."

"There's only one way to find out," Noah said. "We need to find out who this account belongs to and why Jackson's so eager to get his hands on it."

***

As soon as Cat ended the call and placed her phone back in her pocket, she found all four men staring at her.

"Well?" Wyatt asked. "What did they say?"

Cat met his gaze.

"The account belonged to my parents. When they died, it was to be handed over to me on my twenty-fifth birthday."

"Was?" Noah said.

"Apparently the account was drained a few years ago," she answered.

"By whom?" This from Oliver.

"Neil Gallagher," Cat sighed.

Noah swore under his breath.

"Surely there's some of it left somewhere?"

"I don't know. The bank are opening an investigation. If there's anything left, they'll find it."

Her muscles weighing her down, Cat dragged her feet to the sofa a few feet away, fell into the cushioned seat and giggled as Shep jumped onto her lap, begging to be petted.

"What now?" Benjamin said.

It was Noah who answered.

"Now, we hatch a plan."

***

"No! I won't allow it!" Noah shouted, loud enough for the entire floor to hear.

"Why not! I can handle myself! Benjamin's been teaching me self-defence!" Cat cried, jumping from her seat and wincing at the stabbing pain of pins and needles in her feet.

Noah's head swivelled dramatically in his comrade's direction.

"He what?"

"I thought it'd be a good idea, you know, just in case." Benjamin shrugged.

"I can do it, Noah! I know I can! Please, trust me."

Noah sighed heavily, dragging his hand over his face.

"It's too dangerous, Cat. I can't let you be the bait for a crazed serial killer who's out for your blood. You could get hurt."

And he didn't know if he could handle losing someone else – especially someone he had come to love.

"Noah..."

Cat spoke softly as she stepped closer to him, taking his hands in hers.

"I can do this; I know I can. I'm our best shot at catching him."

"But–"

"I'm like a flame in the wind, just like my grandmother's book. The rest of my family – all the other flames – they've all been extinguished. And now, my flame is flickering in the wind – Jackson Moore, threatening to extinguish me too."

Noah closed his eyes and sighed, dreading what he was about to say.

"Okay, but on one condition..."

CHAPTER NINETEEN

"Does everybody understand their roles?" Noah asked his comrades, meeting each of their focused stares, one after the other.

"Yes, Captain," they replied simultaneously.

Noah's heart pounded in his chest. If things went wrong, it wouldn't just be his team on the line – Cat's life was also at stake.

"Good. Let's clue the Chief and the rest of APD in on our op," Noah said, pressing his speed-dial.

Less than fifteen minutes later, Blake Richardson and Evelyn Joy – accompanied by Maria Gonzales – were standing in the hallway to Noah's suite. Noah stared at his boss as he passed by him into the living room. Catching Noah's emotionless stare, Blake arched his eyebrow, but continued over to the group.

"Sit rep," Blake demanded, his arms crossed over his chest.

Wyatt breathed in, preparing to answer, when Noah cut him off.

"What's your history with Dustin Moore?"

Wyatt's mouth shut, but his eyes widened.

Blake showed no reaction to the name.

"I haven't heard that name in years," he said. "Dustin Moore was my first case as part of the K-9 unit in Belmont County ten years ago. Why?"

"Because he mentioned you by name when I went to visit him,". "He said that if it weren't for you, he'd still be out in the world."

. "Me and my dog Diesel were the ones who tracked him down and found the two girls' bodies all those years ago. That man has always blamed me for where he ended up. Other than that, we had no part in the investigation."

"I see. Our killer is Dustin Moore's adoptive son," Noah informed him.

Blake swore under his breath.

"I'm sorry man, I didn't know. Otherwise I would have told you sooner."

"None of us did," Evelyn spoke up. "Why would we?"

After acknowledging Evelyn's words, Noah turned to face the quietest person in the room.

"Maria, is there anything about Jackson we should know – anything we don't know that could lead us to where he could be hiding out now?" he asked.

"I-I don't know. He used to talk about the places his father took him as a child. They travelled around the country." Maria shrugged, not realising that she was giving Noah exactly what he needed. "He showed me pictures, they're–"

Maria's pupils dilated in horror.

"What is it?"

Evelyn turned on her.

"My laptop."

Hastily, Maria dug through her backpack and pulled out a small, colourful laptop. She practically tossed it to Noah, shuddering in disgust as if she had just touched dirt-soaked hair in the shower drain.

"The password is BuckeyeCandies99. The pictures are on it – they're labelled 'Killer Childhood Adventures' – oh God…"

Maria's voice trailed off as she held back a gag and ran into the bathroom, banging the door closed behind her.

"Why didn't we find these before?" Noah demanded, setting the laptop on the table and pressing the power button.

"We only had a warrant for the emails, we couldn't search anything else," Evelyn answered.

Everyone in the room gathered behind Noah as he clicked through each picture – an old farmhouse, the desert, a cemetery.

"They're in the middle of nowhere in each photo," Wyatt whispered.

When Noah reached the final photo, he found himself unable to look away.

"There's something about this photo, but I can't put my finger on what…"

***

Hairs stood on the back of her neck – and on her arms – as she beheld the picture displayed before her eyes. Two men – one older, the other in his late teens – beamed at the camera, eyes smiling, shovels in their hands. Dirt painted their clothes, and their faces were a darker shade than the rest of their exposed skin.

"Oh my God," Cat muttered, and she sprinted into her bedroom, shoving the doors closed after Shep, who had followed her without hesitation. Shaking, she pressed her ear to the door to make out the whispers on the other side.

"Leave her," a voice said. It was Wyatt. "Give her some space to breathe."

Cat knew she didn't have to question who had risen from his seat to come chasing after her. Noah was always there no matter what.

A small whine caught her attention, and Cat turned, still leaning against the door for support, when her legs gave out. Slowly, she slid down to the carpeted floor. Her body trembling, she choked back a cry.

Though she didn't know where Jackson Moore and his father were in those photos, one thing was clear: they were dump sites. The shovels weren't in the Moores' hands in every photo, but Cat found it unlikely that it was a coincidence that there were shovels present in every photo. Whether the others had caught on to the commonality, she wasn't sure.

Her breathing heavy, she lifted her hand to her collar bones, only to remember that she no longer wore her locket. It was evidence now. Who knew when she'd get it back. She closed her eyes but did not count to four. Instead, she thought of her future, and only focused on the positive possibilities.

A new home – one where she wouldn't always

have to watch over her shoulder – where she could make new, happier memories.

A new family.

Noah, Evelyn, hell, even Maria, were her family now, whether she liked it or not. And she could never forget about the guys. She'd come to love them like the older brothers she always wanted, even if she'd only known them a short period of time.

Hope.

Cat had lost count of how many days it had been since she'd arrived in the United States, full of hope and happiness. When she arrived, she knew she'd have the life she'd always wanted. She'd get to go to college, be with her family, create a new life for herself. And though she had lost her grandmother and started off all alone, she knew now that she could still have all those things.

She could be happy.

Cat didn't notice when her breathing had returned to normal. Her thoughts had been elsewhere, planning her future happiness. With a smile smeared across her face, Cat lifted herself from the floor and approached her best friend.

"We'll get through this, boy, and when we do, we'll be happy."

Shep licked her nose in response, causing a soft giggle to escape past her lips.

Moments later, Cat was ready to go back out to the group and face the horror again when her phone buzzed. The caller ID read "Blocked."

Cat answered the phone.

"Hello?"

"Catarina."

A chill ran down Cat's spine, and the hairs stood up on the back of her neck. Her heavy breathing returned, only minutes after she had managed to settle herself.

"What do you want?" she asked.

"You."

His voice was calm, dominant, cold.

"Turn yourself in," Cat said, "and maybe they can cut you a deal."

Cat knew more than anything that Noah would never offer her grandmother's killer a deal. Not in a lifetime. But Jackson didn't know that.

"Meet me at the First Baptist Church in thirty minutes, or I'll kill your precious Detective Thompson the same way I slit dear old Margaret's throat open. And know this: I'm watching you. So, if you even attempt to tell anyone, they're all dead, and it'll be your fault."

Before Cat could say another word, the call ended.

Would he really do it? Would he kill everyone Cat held dear? She didn't want to risk it.

Enough people had died because of her. Jackson was miles ahead of Noah and the APD. They'd never find Jackson without her, and Noah wouldn't let her be the bait unless one of his team were there with her.

It'd never work.

Cat had a choice to make, and she knew exactly what she was going to do.

No one else was going to die because of her.

***

"Cat's been in her room a long time," Noah said to Oliver, who was sitting next to him on the sofa. "I should really go check on her."

He stood up from his seat and rounded the corner to Cat's room, only to find the door open and the dog alone on the bed.

Noah's breath caught in his throat as he scrambled into the room. Frantically, he rushed to the en suite, praying she was sitting on the toilet.

Nothing.

"Where's Cat?" he asked the dog, who got up and pattered from the room.

Noah followed him to the front door of the suite. The dog scratched the door once and lay down on the floor, staring into Noah's eyes with a sad knowing expression.

"No."

Heart racing, Noah rushed back into the living room.

"She's gone" – he struggled for air – "Catarina. She's gone."

CHAPTER TWENTY

Panic rose from Cat's stomach and into her chest as she walked briskly down the road, away from the hotel, away from the safety Noah and his team provided. It had been nearly ten minutes since she had slipped out of the suite unnoticed thanks to the photos of two serial killers which had drawn everyone's undivided attention. Still, Cat had no doubt that Noah had already realised she was missing.

Tears welled in her eyes, threatening to fall at any moment as she thought of the note she had left for Noah in her bedroom.

Had he found it?

There was a chance that she might never know. If she didn't survive this...

Hopefully, he'd take in Shep and give him a home, even though she was well aware that the pair didn't exactly get along.

Cat sniffed back her tears, trying to keep them at bay. Even the smallest shedding of tears could draw a civilian's attention, and that was the last thing she needed – to be found before she'd even reached the church.

Walking down the sidewalk, Cat kept her

head down, when a sudden honk of a car startled her and stopped her in her tracks.

Had someone called her name?

She turned to see a familiar silver car parked across the street, and an unfriendly face peering out at her through the window.

***

Jackson motioned for Catarina to join Him in the car, flashing His teeth as a cool smirk etched across His cheeks. At last, He had her right where He wanted her. All to Himself.

He watched intently as she waited for the road to clear of cars before she approached. Pleasure bubbled in His chest when He noticed her teary-eyed face. That sense of euphoria, however, perished when He managed to get a closer look at His younger cousin.

The locket was gone.

Fury raging within Him, Jackson's expression remained calm until Catarina was seated in the car. He locked the doors and pulled out onto the street.

"What do you want with me?" she asked, but He was sure she already knew the answer.

"Stop playing games," He spat. "Where's the locket?"

As if by habit, Catarina pressed her palm between her collarbones, as if only now remembering that she had not been wearing it.

"I-I don't know—"

"Enough!" Jackson erupted. "We'll deal with

you when we arrive at our final destination."

"We?"

Reaching down beside Him, Jackson pulled His pistol from the side-door pocket and grinned at the *thump* that echoed through the vehicle as the butt of the gun collided with the side of Catarina's head.

***

Noah gripped the handwritten note tightly between his fingers.

How could she do this? Did she not trust their plan?

Did she not trust *him*?

"Where could she have gone?" Benjamin asked, wiping the nervous sweat from his forehead.

Noah had noticed how close Benjamin and Cat had become. He was an only child with a lot of cousins. He'd always wanted a little sister, and it seemed like Cat had fit into that role perfectly.

"I don't know, the note doesn't say," Noah sighed, scratching the back of his neck anxiously. If she was with Jackson already, she didn't have much time.

"She doesn't have the locket with her. Isn't that what Jackson wants? So, if Cat can't give him what he wants..." Wyatt trailed off, unable to finish his sentence without releasing a sob.

Noah had never seen his men so emotional. Cat must have really won over their hearts.

"She's one of us now," Oliver said, as if

reading Noah's thoughts. "We'll find her and get her home safe."

Starting to feel crowded, Noah ordered everybody from the room and back into the living room so they could think of a new plan – one that got Cat home safely.

"Okay, we have the locket. Maria, do you – where's Maria?"

Noah scanned the group of people surrounding him. Maria was nowhere to be found.

"The locket!" he exclaimed, but when he turned to the table where they'd left it, it was gone.

**

"What did you do to her?" a voice called out nearby.

"It's not like I could show her where we were going. Besides, she was asking too many questions," another – Jackson's – voice replied sternly.

Cat's head felt heavy. Pain seared from her temple and spread across her forehead. A vague memory of being hit with the butt of a gun surfaced.

"I didn't sign up for this, Jackson! All those murders... and now *kidnapping*!"

"Enough, Maria! It's too late now! You're in just as much trouble as I am – especially after sending that email. Now, did you bring the locket?"

There was a moment of silence.

"Yes."

Cat's eyelids fluttered open. After taking a moment for her sight to focus, Cat attempted to raise her head. When she lifted her gaze to the two paramedics arguing a few feet away, she felt an unusual strain pulling her shoulders back, arching her back. She wriggled her body, only to realise that her hands were bound behind the back of the chair, and her feet tied together on the floor.

She took a moment to look around her. Dark walls surrounded them, though small broken windows slitted across the walls near the ceiling. Most of the floor was made of tile, except for a few feet of damp soil resting on the opposite side of the room. Cat sniffed. It smelled musty.

"Mm," she moaned, drawing the paramedics' attention to her.

While Jackson gawked at her, a proud smirk on his lips, Maria approached her with care, a bottle of water in her hand.

"Here, drink," she whispered, holding the uncapped bottle to Cat's lips.

Cat watched the woman she thought was her friend suspiciously – how her gentle eyes smiled at her, urging her to take a sip of water. Thirst overcoming her, Cat gulped half the bottle; her dry throat itched. It felt like sandpaper. She licked her lips, ashamed of how desperate she must look as she opened her mouth to drink the water that moistened her tongue. Some of it dripped down her chin and onto her dirty clothes, but she didn't care.

"I have an errand to run. Make sure she doesn't get away," Jackson announced, placing a small peck on Maria's cheek before he disappeared into the darkness.

"Wh-why are you doing this?" Cat asked Maria.

"I didn't sign up for this, Cat. No one was ever supposed to get hurt–"

"Is that what he told you? He's been killing since he was a kid, Maria. He's a psychopath."

"I love him," Maria whined.

Cat met her sad gaze.

"He's not capable of love."

Maria remained speechless for several minutes, taking in Cat's words, and Jackson's actions.

"But if I let you go, he'll kill me," she finally whispered.

Cat shook her head, then immediately regretted the action. Her head thumped worse than any hangover she'd ever seen her uncle go through.

"We won't let him. Noah and his team, they're good at what they do, Maria. They can protect you."

"Promise?"

"Of course."

Maria waited a few more seconds before making her decision. She pulled an army knife from her pocket. Cat leaned forward while Maria rounded the chair and began to work on the ties binding Cat's wrists together. A *snap* echoed through the building, and Cat pulled her hands close to her chest, gently massaging the marks left by the rope. Maria came back around and got to work on the restraints around her ankles.

"What do you think you're doing?" a voice called from an open door on the far side of the room, allowing a shred of light to burst through the opening.

Maria stood up from where she had been crouching at Cat's feet, her hands behind her back.

"I-I-I thought I could trust you!" Jackson bellowed, storming into the room, throwing a shovel to the floor and allowing the door to smack shut behind him.

Maria inched closer to Cat, holding out her army knife within Cat's reach. She wiggled it, hinting for Cat to take it from her grasp. Quickly, Cat took it from her and shoved it into her jeans pocket. Hopefully, she wouldn't need it.

Without warning, Jackson grabbed Maria by the scruff of her neck and rammed her against the nearby wall, raising her up so that her feet were dangling inches above the ground. Maria scratched at his arm, silently begging him to let her go. Cat watched in horror, unable to release the air frozen in her lungs as Maria gasped for air, her face whitening the longer he held her there.

Terror reflected in Maria's eyes as she looked to Cat, who sat rooted to the chair, tears falling over her cheeks.

***

"I can't believe Maria could be in on it too. She was such a sweet girl," Evelyn ranted as she sat in front of the open laptop, scanning each photo one by one.

Hatred coursed through Noah's veins. It boiled in his stomach, surged in his chest. He had trusted Maria. She was Cat's friend. She'd been so kind to Cat all this time.

Why would she do something so stupid?

"Well, she is. We just have to deal with it and try to find Cat before it's too late. She's already been missing for three hours," Noah said, leaning over the chair behind his partner and examining the photos.

A second pair of eyes couldn't hurt. Blake had returned to the station to send officers out to the streets. Hopefully, someone would spot Jackson or Maria somewhere and they'd have an idea on where to start looking.

Evelyn clicked through each photo, taking her time scouring everyone to find as many details as possible that could help them. It was only when they reached the final photo that Noah made the connection.

"Holy…"

Evelyn swerved around to face Noah, a curious glint in her eyes.

"What?"

"Killer Childhood Adventures," Noah whispered.

Evelyn nudged him, hoping for more information.

"Go through each photo again. How many years do they span?"

"About ten or so," Evelyn answered.

"And what's the commonality in each photo?" Noah said.

Evelyn clicked through each photo again, this time quicker than the last.

"Oh my God. How did we not see this before?"

"Because we weren't looking at the backgrounds," Noah answered.

In each photo, a shovel could be seen in the background. After looking closer, there was also a sign in each relating back to a particular state or county.

"What have we got?" Blake said, bursting through the door and into the suite.

"The photos, they're dumpsites," Noah said, moving out of the way so Blake could see. "It explains why there's a shovel in every photo – and they always look like they've just been used. See there, the fresh dirt on the bottom?" Noah pointed a finger at the shovels resting against the wall in the final photo.

"Hold on a second..." Blake started.

He crouched down beside Evelyn and pulled the laptop closer to him.

"Detective Joy, zoom in on the top right corner there," he said, his focus now completely on the corner of the photo.

Evelyn did as Blake ordered, which resulted in an unusual gasp from her boss.

"I know it. I know this place. This is where we

found the Clairsville Twins," Blake whispered.

Noah's heart dropped in his chest and suddenly the air became heavy. He reached out for the table to steady himself, only to find one of his comrades holding him up.

"Cap?" Oliver questioned, a worried look in his eyes.

Noah nodded to the medic, who led him to the nearby sofa.

"What is it?" Blake said.

"He's bringing her back to where it all ended for him and his father. To the last piece of happiness he had before his father was arrested and he found out his true identity." Noah sucked in a full breath of air, sweat accumulating on his forehead. "We have to get to St. Clairsville."

CHAPTER TWENTY-ONE

Patrol cars fled the station's car park and onto the street as Noah stepped out of the SUV. The sun kissed his face when he turned, waiting for the rest of his team to exit the vehicle and follow him into the local station of St. Clairsville, Ohio.

It had taken two hours to get here – two hours that Cat may not have had. But Noah could not think that way. Not if he wanted to remain focused and on task for the rescue mission.

The station's air con cooled his skin as he rammed his way past the front desk and into the bull pen.

"Where can we set up, Detective?" he asked the lanky man walking towards him in an expensive grey suit.

"This way."

The detective swerved in his steps and led Noah and his team to a large office area obviously meant for daily debriefings. Noah wasted no time. As soon as he was through the door he set blueprints on the table, with a map of the local area next to them, markers labelling the building where they suspected Cat was being held.

Wyatt followed closely behind, Oliver on his heels. As they rounded the table, their weapons were in their hands. By habit, each man had drawn their weapon of choice, ensured that their magazines were loaded, and wracked the slides. Once they were all satisfied with their checks, Noah, Oliver, and Wyatt geared up.

Benjamin, who was already geared up with a rifle bag slung over his shoulder, entered the room, a deadly grin on his face.

"Let's get this bastard," he said.

Noah nodded wholeheartedly and motioned for his unit to huddle around the table.

"Benjamin, I need you on this roof to the south of the building. There's a big enough window there so you'll be able to view the main hall." A melancholy frown passed over Noah's face at his next words before he quickly regained himself. "Our team doesn't have a spotter, so Blake will be fulfilling that role for this op."

Blake strode into the room dressed in his gear, a hint of a smirk on his face.

"Does this mean I'm an honorary member of Phantom now?"

"You wish," Wyatt laughed.

Noah allowed his men a brief moment of laughter before pulling them back on task.

"Wyatt, how many explosives do you have?" he asked.

"Enough." Wyatt smirked, pride in his eye.

"Right. Rig every exit except the entrance on the south side with a small detonation. Enough to injure, not enough to kill. That will be our point of entry and escape."

Wyatt nodded, already getting to work on the small traps.

"What about me, Cap?" Oliver said, watching his Captain closely.

"You're with me," Noah answered. "I'm going to need someone to watch my six and, God forbid, if Cat's injured... well, I can't think of any better man for the job."

At that, the local detective re-joined Noah's team in the debriefing room.

"Roadblocks set up. You're good to go."

Noah acknowledged the detective's news with a grunt, then met each of his comrades' gazes and said, "Let's go to work, men."

***

Cat watched Jackson pat down the soil with the back of the shovel. Where it had once stretched flat across the ground, there was now a large mound. Tears flowed down Cat's cheeks, the image of Maria's listless body being covered in dirt at the forefront of her mind.

"Why did you do that? Why did you kill her?" Cat cried.

"She betrayed me. I loved her and she betrayed me."

While Jackson's attention remained on the new grave, Cat plucked the knife from her pocket and began to cut the ties around her ankles.

In all his hastiness, Jackson had forgotten to bind her hands back together.

Cat prayed that he didn't turn his attention back to her before she managed to free herself, and she dared not say another word, for the risk that he would.

The ties snapped, and Cat caught her breath, jerking her head up momentarily at her captor. But Jackson had not noticed. His attention was still on his partner, whom he had just killed.

A door stood to her left. Where it led, Cat wasn't sure. But it would get her away from Jackson, away from the impending death that awaited her, too.

Still sitting in the chair, Cat readied herself for a task she was not well acquainted with: running. As she took in a deep breath, however, Jackson turned to her, and advanced. Realising she was free, he didn't even take the time to react.

Cat had to move.

Now.

"She's dead because of you!" he cried, fury burning in his eyes.

Jackson pulled back his fist, intending on delivering a blow to Cat's body. For a fraction of a second, Cat found herself glued to the ground, allowing the fear of this man to overpower her.

For years, she had allowed a man to abuse her – to hit her, punch her, kick her, push her around. She was done being afraid, and this was the perfect chance to face her fears.

Jackson may have been stronger than her, but she was smaller – and faster.

Cat ducked to the left, dodging Jackson's blow, and landed on her left foot. Just as

Benjamin had taught her, she leaned into her left side and kicked her other foot into Jackson's abdomen.

"You bitch!" he screamed through the pain, almost doubling over as he pressed his arms across his stomach.

Taking the opportunity, Cat fisted her right hand and delivered a strong right hook, connecting with Jackson's nose. This time, however, she didn't wait to watch his reaction. Now was her only opportunity to run.

With speed she didn't know she had, she rushed through the side door and into a room enveloped in darkness.

***

"All explosives are rigged and ready to go," Wyatt announced through Noah's headset.

Noah watched the abandoned building, peering through his binoculars, ensuring everything was quiet.

"Copy," he said. "Circle the perimeter, make sure nobody comes in or out."

"Aye aye, Captain."

"Benjamin, Blake, sit rep."

"In position. No sign of movement in the main hall, the other rooms are darker, can't see much," Benjamin answered.

"We'll find them, don't you worry," Blake added.

Noah peeled the binoculars from his eyes and faced his right-hand man.

"Ready?"

Oliver nodded his head, throwing his med kit over his shoulder and drawing his weapon.

"Let's go."

***

Her breath heavy, Cat navigated her way through the many rooms of the building. There had to be a way out somewhere, but it was so dark, she found herself unable to see past a few feet ahead of her at a time.

"Catarina... There's nowhere for you to hide. I will find you," Jackson called eerily into the darkness.

Cat covered her mouth – an attempt to muffle the sob that had slipped past her lips. The rattling of a locked door taunted her thoughts. Each door she had managed to find was the same. Locked.

She turned, only to find herself back where she had started. The door she had come through minutes ago allowed a few splashes of light to illuminate her path. A glint of metal caught her attention, if only for a moment, and a new sense of hope surged through her.

Another door.

"Where are you, little cousin?"

Cat ran to the door, her lungs empty of air, and pulled on the handle.

A small boom erupted around her, sending the door flying off its hinges and shattering the wall. Cat felt her back slam against the wall behind her.

CHAPTER TWENTY-TWO

"Did you hear that?" Noah asked Oliver, holding his fist in the air. The two men stopped in their tracks, stunted by the small explosion emanating from the back of the building.

"I'm on it, Cap. You keep going. Find Cat," Wyatt informed him.

Though Noah knew there was a possibility a small animal might have set off the explosion, he felt as though something had happened to Cat. Reluctantly, he lowered his fist, and they continued on track to the side entrance of the building.

"Captain, we have eyes on Jackson and Cat." Benjamin's unsteady tone only confirmed Noah's suspicions.

"Tell me."

"Jackson's dragging her back into the main hall. Something's wrong. Her clothes are black, her hair is static. She doesn't look steady on her feet."

"Do you have a clean shot on Jackson?"

"Negative."

Noah's heart sank, giving anxiety enough

time to rise to the surface.

"Where are they?" he asked his comrade.

"Back left corner, near the source of the explosion. He's holding her against the wall, Noah, and he's got a gun."

Noah's stomach plunged, and though he felt like he might be sick, he said, "We're going in."

***

The deafening ringing in Cat's ears muffled Jackson's words. Pain coursed through her head, and, for some odd reason, her neck hurt. Cat's eyes lurched open; her hands instinctively clawed at Jackson's arm, which was pressed tightly against her throat, depriving her of air.

"As I was saying" – he enunciated each word carefully – "that money should have been mine all along. The money is to be given to the eldest Gallagher child. That would be me. So where do you think you get off taking it for yourself, hmm?"

"I... don't... have... it," Cat breathed out.

Jackson tightened his hold around her throat again.

"What do you mean you don't have it! I checked the account, everything's gone!" he shouted, anger filling his voice.

"Neil... took it."

Cat's words only seemed to enrage her cousin more as he released his hold around her throat, only to point a gun at her heart. Though her lungs begged her for air, Cat was paralysed, her breath caught in her throat.

"After all this time, and the money isn't even there." Jackson switched off the safety. "Well, I guess I have no need for you anymore. Goodbye, little cousin."

***

"Jackson Moore, put your hands up where I can see them!"

Heart pounding in his chest, Noah watched Jackson flick the safety off and aim his weapon close to Cat's heart. His breath quickened at the thought of failing – of losing yet another loved one.

Noah caught Cat's miserable gaze before Jackson twisted, dragging her in front of him, his arm holding her in a lock and blocking Noah's shot.

"Move and I'll kill her," Jackson spat.

"Don't do it, Jackson," Noah said, steadying his voice.

Jackson raised the gun until the muzzle pressed against Cat's temple. It was obvious that Cat was trying not to squirm under the man's grip, but Noah didn't know how long she could hold out for.

"Captain, I have a clear shot. Permission to take it?" Benjamin's voice rang over the headset.

"Negative," Noah whispered. "Not until the hostage is cleared."

"You know this bitch got everything I never did? Money, a home, a family – all of it," Jackson started. "Instead, I was abandoned, abused, neglected." He smirked. "That is, until daddy dearest took me in. He taught me how to be strong – how to take what I wanted."

"He taught you how to be a monster," Cat hissed.

"Shut up!"

"You know," Cat continued, "my parents wanted to adopt you."

If Noah had witnessed Cat's bravery in this situation a week ago, he'd have never believed his eyes. Now, it only made him love her even more.

"Rubbish!" Jackson cried, pressing the gun harder against the side of her head. Noah made a move to step forward.

"I said don't move!"

"Okay! Okay!" Noah said, raising his arms in the air and slowly crouching to the ground.

"What are you doing?" Oliver whispered angrily at his superior.

Noah laid his gun on the ground and kicked it away.

"She's telling the truth, you know. The Gallaghers wanted to take you in as their own. They even contacted Dustin, arranged to meet him and Meredith."

"Bullshit."

"That's when they died," Cat said softly. "They died trying to get to you. You were supposed to be my big brother."

A moment's hesitation. That's all they needed.

***

At those last words, Jackson loosened his grip around her body, leaving an opening for escape. Effortlessly, Cat slipped her hand into her pocket and drew Maria's army knife.

Jackson sucked in a breath.

"This is not how I would have liked to watch you die."

"No!" Noah shouted, distracting Jackson long enough for Cat to stab him in the arm and push out from under his grip.

Cat had just escaped Jackson's clutches when a thundering bang echoed around the room behind her.

Cat flinched at the sound, preparing for impact, but the pain never came. Another shot rang in her ears as she turned around just in time to watch Jackson Moore fall to the ground, blood oozing from his mouth, and Wyatt standing behind him, gun poised.

As Cat turned around, she expected to find Noah standing there with an accomplished grin on his face. Instead, she found the man she'd come to love lying on the cold, hard ground, in a pool of his own blood, and Oliver leaning over him.

"NOAH!"

CHAPTER TWENTY-THREE

Cat arched her back in the chair, sighing in relief as her muscles stretched, releasing the tension in the knots surrounding her shoulders. It had been three days since Noah was shot.

"He's not out of the woods yet," one of the doctors had told her after his four-hour surgery.

The bullet had entered his shoulder and lodged itself mere inches from his heart.

He had saved her. The bullet he took – the one Jackson had fired – had been aimed at her. Noah had jumped in front of her to save her, and she hadn't even realised it until after he was down.

Guilt had blanketed Cat in the days following the shooting. Jackson was dead, and she should be happy, but until Noah – the only true family she had left – was healthy again, she couldn't bring herself to find joy in her life. Not yet.

Cat had not let go of Noah's hand since she'd woken up that morning. So, at the smallest twitch of his finger, a jolt of newfound energy surged through her body.

"Noah? Noah, are you awake?" she whispered.

Another twitch and, slowly, Noah's eyes began to flutter open.

"Hey sweetheart," he smiled.

"Noah!"

Cat jumped from her chair and wrapped her arms around him. Noah winced, and Cat quickly regretted her actions.

"Sorry."

"It's okay. I'm so happy you're okay," Noah said, still smiling.

Cat sat on the edge of the bed, careful not to lean on Noah's aching body.

"I'll always be okay whenever you're around. Just don't ever do something stupid like that again."

"Cat..."

"No. No 'Cat'. You can't die on me, Noah Thompson. Not ever."

Eyes tearing up, Cat stared at the man she'd only met a week ago and wondered how she could ever be scared of men as long as Noah was around. He truly was the perfect man.

"Hey now."

Noah lifted his hand and gently caressed Cat's cheek, moving on to brush his fingers through her hair.

"Noah..."

"It's okay."

Cat leaned closer, refusing to look away from the mesmerising blue eyes that had first captured her attention back in Ireland.

She rested her palm on Noah's cheek and hovered over his body.

Slowly, she lowered herself, closing her eyes. Her heart beat thunderously in her chest, and butterflies fluttered in her stomach.

Noah's soft lips brushed against hers, his touch gentle and sweet. Her eyes closed, Cat leaned deeper into the kiss, which Noah welcomed enthusiastically.

Then came a knock on the door.

"Hey, Cat, we got you – oh uhh..."

Benjamin's voice trailed off at the sight of Cat and his Captain on the bed. Cat pulled away from Noah, and made to seat herself back in the chair, but Noah took her hand and shook his head.

"It's okay," he said again.

Cat remained sitting on the bed, her fingers intertwined with Noah's, and watched the members of Phantom enter the room, each holding a container.

While Benjamin and Oliver remained silent, Wyatt took the opportunity to comment.

"Well, it's about freaking time." He whistled, winking at Noah. "Who made the first move?"

"Shut up, Grey," Noah laughed, momentarily forgetting his wounds, and flinching from the pain.

"What do you have there?"

Cat nodded at the containers in her new friends' hands.

"Oh, we have brownies, cupcakes and scones. Want some?"

Cat nodded her head enthusiastically, only

now realising that she hadn't eaten since the morning before.

"Thank you," she said, taking a jam scone from Oliver's container.

She began to munch at her breakfast, listening to the men tell stories of their time in Afghanistan and their lives since they'd returned.

"So," Wyatt began. "What's going to happen now, Cat?"

Cat met Noah's gaze, a mischievous smile on her lips.

"That's entirely up to Noah."

***

Six weeks later

Sweat dripped down Cat's forehead as she handed the last of the boxes to Noah, who stood on the back of the jeep.

"That's all of them," she told him, using the back of her hand to block the sun from her eyes.

Noah jumped down from the jeep and wrapped his arm around her back.

"Well, Miss Gallagher, we better get you and this dog here to your new home. You don't want to miss your first day of this internship of yours."

Cat laughed, though she couldn't help but feel nervous. She'd always wanted to be a writer, and when she'd received word from the local publisher that her grandmother had written a letter concerning a paid internship with the company, she couldn't help but think Margaret O'Donnell was helping her from beyond the grave.

"Do you think they'll like me?" she asked her new boyfriend anxiously.

"Sweetheart, I know they will. Who wouldn't love a girl like you? But be warned, if any of them try to make a move on you, Phantom will be ready to go."

Cat's boisterous laugh filled the cabin of the SUV. For the first time in a very long time, she was happy.

"I love you, Noah Thompson."

Noah's eyes glistened in the sun at her words.

"I love you too, Catarina Gallagher. And I always will."

About the Author

Lauren Hanney was born and raised in Dublin, Ireland, before moving to County Meath when she was six. From a young age, you would always find a book in her hand, whether she was walking to school or at home cuddled up with the latest Jacqueline Wilson novel. As she grew older, her taste in books changed. Today, she'll tell you her favourite author is Agatha Christie, and you'll never find her without a good mystery in her bag. Now, Lauren is a student of Maynooth University with a passion for English and hopes to pursue a career in the writing industry after graduation. When she's not out spending time with friends and family, you can find her at home writing whatever project she's currently working on.

If you want to know what Lauren's currently working on, visit her website today at www.laurenhanney.com and subscribe to her newsletter for the latest updates.

You can connect with her on:

Twitter: @thelaurenhanney

Facebook: @thelaurenhanney

Instagram: @thelaurenhanney